SURPRISE ATTACK!

Jess walked back to the edge facing the flat, looked down at the approaching cavalry column, moving slowly toward him across the deep sands. He started to raise his arm, to wave them on to the butte.

At that moment the sand on both sides of the column erupted. Mounds of sand flew up and aside with the blankets they'd covered, revealing the heads, shoulders, arms, and aimed rifles of thirty Apache warriors, fifteen on each side of the trapped column.

Thirty rifles crashed in a ragged, point-blank volley, their bullets smashing into the stunned cavalrymen.

And while screams, yells, and meshed reports of the first slaughtering barrage still hung in the air, fifteen mounted Chiricahua warriors came howling out of the mouth of the nearest canyon and thundered head-on against McAllister's decimated command. . . .

Also by Marvin Albert:

THE UNTOUCHABLES

Stone Angel Novels
Published by Fawcett Books:

STONE ANGEL

BACK IN THE REAL WORLD

GET OFF AT BABYLON

LONG TEETH

APACHE RISING

Marvin H. Albert

FAWCETT GOLD MEDAL • NEW YORK

A Fawcett Gold Medal Book
Published by Ballantine Books
Copyright © 1957 by Marvin H. Albert

ISBN 0-449-13361-3

The characters in this book are entirely imaginary and have no relation to
any living person.

Manufactured in the United States of America

First Ballantine Books Edition: January 1988

ONE

Stones rattled above Jess Remsberg's head, rolled down the shale overhang under which he rode his coyote dun horse at a walk. The stones, small ones, rolled over the lip of the overhang, fell past Jess with a fine sprinkling of dust, and went on rolling down the slope below him. Jeff grabbed a fistful of Lobo's black mane and tightened gently, warning the dun to be still.

Lobo froze like a statue in the shadow of the shale overhang. His fine head came up, wide nostrils flaring at the sudden scent of danger. Jess Remsberg stared out into the dazzling glare, his wide gray eyes narrowed against the acid bite of the hot dust.

The land for miles around, as far as he could see, was fashioned out of a monstrous mass of stone, carved, twisted and eroded into tortured spires and jagged bone-dry gullies blanketed with sand and the haze of alkali dust. Nothing moved in that land unless something moved it, and there was no wind.

Jess strained to hear any sound above him. None came. No more stones rolled over his protective overhang. His ears were stuffed with the enormous silence. A trickle of moisture slid down his long spine.

Though he'd ridden slowly for the past three hours, ever since finding the lone figure staked out spread-eagled on that sand hill, Jess was panting. It was the heavy, crushing weight of the heat that did that, and the inevitable spasms of fear.

1

That man on the sand hill had been burned to death the slow Apache way. First the flesh of one hand and arm consumed by the fire, then the other. Then the feet and the legs. Last a small fire placed on the still-heaving chest to burn down inside and consume the beating heart. It took hours, and the Apaches knew how to keep a man hideously conscious through it all, right up to the blessed end.

The buzzards had been at the corpse for more than an hour when Jess Remsberg reached the place. Claws and beaks had torn at the flesh, plucked out the eyes. But the purple birthmark on the cheek of the corpse carried Jess back across a year of bitter memories to an army scout named Tom Van, a cunning Dutchman who'd thought his way through hostiles for twenty years, from Canada clear down to Mexico. Van's luck and cleverness had run out here, in this land of pink-and-brown stone.

Jess was safely hidden where he was. The shape of his dun horse and of his own tall, thin figure, merged into the shadow of the overhang. Jess's patched boots, Levis, denim work jacket and battered Stetson were dust-caked to the color of his horse, blending with the stone and the shimmering heat-haze. From more than fifty yards away, no eyes could pick him out as long as he remained there—not even keen, patient Apache eyes. And no further sounds had reached his straining ears since those stones had rolled down the shale.

But he couldn't stop the surges of fear from running through him with the pulsing of his blood.

He pulled the yellow-and-brown neckerchief down away from his nostrils and mouth, tasted sparingly of the warm water that remained in one of his two canteens. The other canteen had been empty since sunup.

The liquid fought its way through the dust caking his tongue and throat. Capping the canteen, he reached for the neckerchief to pull it back up as a dust shield. His hand froze before it touched the neckerchief.

A dark speck moved on the rimrock a mile away across the vast, boxed-in canyon.

The nerves of Jess Remsberg's stomach jerked. That speck must have been moving out there in the open for some time, but it hadn't caught his eyes till it was outlined briefly against the pink of a distant sandstone tower. Jess eased the carbine out of his saddle boot and rested it across the pommel in front of him, his fingers tense against the trigger guard.

The dark speck moved slowly along the rimrock, coming toward him but still too far off to make out.

Jess longed for the makings of a cigarette. Not to light up and smoke, but just to hold between his lean lips and taste the tobacco with the tip of his tongue. Smoking was a strong habit with him. Stronger even than liquor, for the liquor was a more recent thing.

But he'd deliberately left both the makings and the liquor behind him when he set out on this long ride in response to McAllister's mysteriously urgent message. Indulging a habit calmed a man's nerves, but out here it was better not to be calm.

You seldom got to see Apaches before they jumped you. Sometimes you couldn't even find their sign when they were all around you. You had to sense when they were there, be able to feel the strange warning quiver of nerve ends keyed to almost unbearable tension—the way his nerves were quivering now.

The dark speck came closer slowly, grew gradually into the shape of a horse and a rider. Jess stayed where he was, nothing about him moving but the long thin fingers of his right hand stroking the trigger guard of his carbine.

His slitted gray eyes watched. His bony, flat-planed face was taut, alert, but it held nothing of the fear jangling inside him, as though the part of his mind that controlled his face knew nothing of that fear, or coldly ignored it.

His face was that of a man in his early thirties; big-nosed, wide-mouthed, lean and hard as the rest of him. Time and weather had worked at it, toughening and darkening it. The gray of his watching eyes was startling in the leathery darkness of that face.

The horse and rider came through the shadow between two sandstone columns and emerged again into the pitiless sunlight. A pulse quickened in Jess's throat. The wide-brimmed hat and checkered shirt were those of a man. But now the rider was close enough for Jess to see the split riding skirt, long and buckskin-colored. The rider was a woman.

Jess raised his head quickly, his slitted eyes searching. Nothing moved anywhere in that pink-and-brown tangle but that single horse and rider. But still Jess did not move. He remained in the protective patch of shadow, watching, waiting.

The horse, faltering with each step, suddenly stopped, and then fell forward to its knees. The rider wrenched herself free of the saddle before the horse fell over on its side.

For long minutes they remained that way, motionless, the large dark shape of the horse stretched out on its side and the smaller figure of the woman standing a few feet away, looking down at the horse.

Then the woman began walking, leaving the horse behind, still coming on in Jess Remsberg's direction. She staggered, unable to walk in a straight line. Jess sucked his lips between his teeth and bit down gently, holding himself where he was with a jolt of instinct-driven will power.

He watched her slowly climb a mound of loose shale that blocked her path. At the top, she halted, her head hanging down. She stood there for a moment, swaying, and then abruptly sat down.

Stones rattled down the rock slope to the left of Jess. He turned his head quickly. Two pony-riding Indians emerged from their hiding place around a shoulder in the same wall that sheltered Jess, not more than two hundred yards away. They wore the tall black hats of reservation Indians, but their dark faces, upper arms and exposed chests were smeared with stripes of bright paint. Chiricahua Apache war paint. Each carried a rifle.

The two warriors rode down the rock slope toward the woman hunched over on top of the shale mound.

The nervous fear left Jess as soon as he saw them, as it always did, once he knew where they were. A coldness took its place within him. He levered a load into the chamber of his carbine, the click echoing and re-echoing loudly against the walls of the canyon.

The two Apaches reined up instantly, as though halted by the same invisible hand, and swerved toward the alien sound. Jess's first shot slammed into the white stripe across the chest of the one to the left, and drove him backward off his pony. The other Apache kicked his mount and raced back toward the shoulder of the cliff, aiming to circle around behind Jess.

Jess levered a fresh load into the chamber. The Apache had swung down on the other side of his galloping pony, offering only his brown leg over its back as a target. Jess chose the bigger target instead, aiming quickly and squeezing the trigger. The flat blast of the shot drummed back at him from the walls and spires of stone, and the pony went down with a scream. Its rider flung himself free as it fell, scrambled to his feet still clutching his rifle, and sprinted toward a protective jut of rock.

Jess levered and aimed at the crouched, weaving runner, and fired just as the Apache threw himself behind the rock. The carbine slug whined off the top of the rock, throwing up a shower of dust.

Jess waited. The Apache did not show himself. Minutes slid silently by. From behind the rock came a high-pitched call. Jess, understanding, jerked his head around to the right. Two hundred yards away, the unharmed pony of the dead Apache raised its head and looked toward the rock.

The hidden warrior cried out again. The pony whickered, pawed the dust, and began slowly trotting toward the rock. Jess hated to do it, but there was no way he could get to that pony without passing the jut of rock and taking a shot from the Apache crouched behind it. He raised his carbine, aimed at the pony's head, and fired. The pony went forward on its knees and then collapsed on its side. Its head flogged the ground. Jess levered another shell into the chamber and fired again. The pony lay still.

Jess watched the rock as he rammed fresh loads into the carbine. When the Apache didn't show himself, Jess kneed Lobo out of the shadow and raced down the slope to the woman.

She still sat atop the shale, her slim figure sagging forward in an arc of exhaustion. Her head came up as he reached her, big green eyes staring at him. But the eyes were dazed, and he knew she saw no more than the vague shape of a man on a horse. She said, "Leave me be." The way the words rasped out of her, he could tell her mouth was dry and caked with dust.

She didn't rise when he slipped quickly out of his saddle beside her. He saw that she couldn't. Her wide-boned, freckled face was masked with dust. So was her dark red hair, where it was gathered at the back of her neck under the wide-brim hat in a big bun that was coming apart in straggly ends. She seemed to be in her early twenties, but the roasting sun had gotten to her insides and had steamed out the last ounce of young vitality.

When he crouched beside her, reaching for her, she shrank back. "Do not harm me," she whispered raggedly. "I am Flame."

It shocked him for a moment—the words she'd spoken were pure Apache!

Then he grabbed her shoulders. "Don't be scared," he told her. "I'm no Indian."

This time the rasping words were in English: "Leave me be."

"There're Apaches in these hills," he snapped at her. "They get you, they'll kill you. Or worse."

"They won't kill me," she whispered harshly.

Impatiently, Jess yanked her to her feet. She didn't resist. But her legs bore little of her weight. Most of it hung limply in his grip. Her mouth was open, her breath dragging past her teeth and swollen tongue.

Jess managed to shove her up across Lobo in front of the saddlehorn like a sack of meal. He got the toe of his boot into the stirrup and swung up. Something stung his cheek as he settled in the saddle. The crack of a rifle mingled with the slap and whine of a bullet ricocheting off the rocks. Echoes of the shot beat down on them from the eroded walls of the canyon. Jess raked the dun horse with his spurs.

He had difficulty holding the girl's limp body on the horse as they raced back up the slope. Somewhere behind them the rifle blasted again. Jess saw dust spurt from the slope a few feet ahead of them. He felt blood trickling down his cheek from the cut of the first bullet. Then they were over the rim and into the protection of a forest of sandstone boulders.

The half-conscious girl in front of him needed water badly. He glanced at the sky. It was a long way to dark.

That Chiricahua warrior couldn't catch them afoot, but there was no way of knowing how many more there were, somewhere in this enormous maze of stone. The sound of rifle fire carried for miles in land like this, and Jess couldn't outrace Apache ponies with his horse carrying double.

He threaded Lobo through the boulders, circling toward the highest rock formations in the area. When he had put about seven miles between them and the horseless Apache, they reached the side of a big butte. He circled till he found a narrow shelf forming a pathway up along the wall. Lobo struggled up it, slipping dangerously once on loose shale, until they reached the boulders at the top.

It would have to do. Jess urged Lobo into the shadows. He slid out of the saddle, then eased the girl down to the ground, propping her in a sitting position against the side of a boulder. Getting the canteen that was still half full, he offered it to her. The girl's dust-filmed eyes were open, but she made no move to reach for the canteen. Her arms hung at her sides, and he could see her tongue pressed against her bared teeth.

Placing the canteen on her lap, Jess drew his carbine out of its scabbard, made sure there was a fresh load in the chamber, and gave his attention to the tangle of rocks below them. He studied every shadowed hiding place he could see for a full ten minutes without detecting any sign of movement.

Jess glanced back at the girl. The canteen still lay in her

lap. Placing his carbine near the lip of the ledge, Jess crawled over to her, careful not to expose himself to a shot from below. Unscrewing the cap from the canteen, he sank his fingers into the heavy mass of dark red hair at the back of her neck and braced her head. Her glazed green eyes stared upward at nothing. Jess forced the mouth of the canteen against her teeth and tilted, letting the water trickle into her mouth.

She gasped, then made a strangling sound, her head jerking in his grip. He took the canteen away and raised her head till she stopped choking. Her eyes suddenly closed and the tip of her tongue crept out between her teeth to lick drops of water from her dust-caked lips. A low moan escaped her.

Her hat had fallen back, exposing a short, wide scar on her forehead at the hairline. The scar was not more than a couple of months old.

He put the canteen to her mouth again. This time she drank greedily. He let her have almost half a cupful before pulling the canteen away. She moved again, her eyes opening, focusing on his face.

She murmured harshly, "I turned back . . . I wanted to go to him . . . But I became afraid . . . I turned back . . ."

Jess couldn't make sense of it. He decided she was raving from the effects of being out in that sun too long.

"Listen," he whispered urgently. "Where are you from?"

For a few seconds, he thought she wasn't going to speak again. But then she said, "Avalanche."

Avalanche. That was the little settlement outside Fort Creel, the army post where McAllister was waiting for Jess. More than sixty miles to the north—sixty miles of emptiness.

"What are you doing out here?" he asked her.

She stared at him blankly. Then her eyes flickered and she murmured: "I tried . . . but I was afraid . . . I was afraid to go back . . ."

Jess stared at her, confused. When she closed her eyes

suddenly and slumped back, sighing, he eased her over till she lay on her side. Her breathing became heavier, steadier. He picked up the canteen.

Later, he'd give her more water, and some of the dried beef and biscuit from his food bag. For the moment, this would have to do. Her insides had some moisture to absorb, and she was in the shade. He went to Lobo, uncapped the canteen again, and let the dun lap a few handfuls of water. Jess drank last, and when he was done there wasn't much water left.

He hung the canteen from his saddle and went back to his carbine at the lip of the shelf. He looked at the sleeping girl again, wondering what she was doing alone in the middle of this dangerous, empty land, sixty miles from the nearest white settlement.

He found himself thinking of another girl of about the same age who'd ridden alone out through savage emptiness much like this—coming after Jess, and finding a violent death instead. Singing Sky; her name rose to his lips and he spoke it silently, feeling the thin edge of a distant grief still sharp within him.

But that girl had been a Comanche. The land through which she'd been riding when she was murdered was her land, familiar to her. This was a redhaired white girl. She could have no business out here alone.

There were no answers to be had from staring at her. Jess turned his back to her, crawled forward till he could squint over the edge of the shelf. He began again to study the tangle of rocks stretching out below.

There were about three hours left until dark. He looked up at the distant purple humps of the hills to the northeast. There was water to be found there, in potholes sheltered from the sun, where rainwater was held for weeks, the only place he could obtain water for the last leg of his ride to Fort Creel.

But the Apaches knew those water holes as well as Jess. The nearer he got to them, the more likelihood there was of running into a band of them. From here on, he could move only by night.

Behind him, the girl was muttering something. He put the carbine down and went to her. She lay the way he'd placed her, eyes still shut. But her arms and legs moved restlessly, as though fighting something in her sleep.

Her dry lips were parted, moving. He knelt down to hear her. The words came haltingly, harshly: "My son . . . I want my son . . ."

Jess sat back on his boot heels and stared down at her. In her sleep, she was speaking the language of the Chiricahua Apaches.

It was an hour after dawn, two days later, when Lobo carried them into the little adobe town of Avalanche. Jess was in the saddle, the girl behind him, her arms around his waist for balance. Jess felt the warmth of her body against his back, her breath hot on his neck, and he experienced a sense of closeness to her that was not entirely physical.

He had learned practically nothing about her in the two days since finding her. She'd hardly spoken during the whole time, and her silence was a wall between her and the world.

He'd learned that her name was Ellen Graff, and that her husband was a freighter with a new warehouse in Avalanche. Nothing else. She hadn't volunteered an explanation of what she was doing when he found her, and he hadn't asked her after that first time. She hadn't spoken again in the tongue of the Apaches, and he hadn't mentioned it to her.

For there was in her manner something he recognized as akin to his own. An air of private defeat. A lonely pride that fended off intrusion into her solitary being. He wondered about her, but he did not pry.

As they neared a small adobe house, she said suddenly: "There. That's it."

He brought Lobo to a halt. Jess slid out of the saddle and helped Ellen Graff to dismount. She stood beside the dun horse, staring at the house, not moving toward it. Her green eyes shone darkly with cold misery.

Jess limped to the door of the building and banged on it.

After a minute, the door was opened by a bleary-eyed man buckling the belt of his pants with one hand. He was big and burly-shouldered, his handsome face deeply tanned from the sun. He was in his late twenties.

Millard Graff looked sleepily at Jess, then past him to his wife. He didn't look very surprised. Mostly, he looked resigned.

"So you're back," Millard Graff stated flatly, his voice thick with sleep.

Ellen Graff said nothing. After a moment, she advanced toward the door with slow, heavy steps. She stopped beside Jess. The man and his wife looked into each other's eyes without expression. When Millard Graff stood aside at last, she walked past him and disappeared into the gloom inside, not looking back at Jess.

Millard Graff cleared his throat and said quietly to Jess: "You the one found her?"

Jess nodded, trying to comprehend the strangeness of this, and failing. He was unable to understand either of their attitudes.

"Where's the horse?" Millard Graff asked him, a harsh note in his voice.

"Dead."

The muscles of the freighter's face clenched. "And she's back," he rasped. "Should have been the other way. The horse was worth . . ."

Millard Graff's eyes dropped before Jess's stare. The freighter's face darkened with shame and it was plain he wished he hadn't spoken so.

"Thanks for bringing her back," he mumbled, and quickly backed up and closed the door in Jess's amazed face.

Jess stood there for a few seconds, staring at the closed door. Then he shook his head to clear it of confusion.

He turned and limped back to Lobo, led the horse down the empty dirt street toward the stable and town corral.

He needed a drink, bad.

TWO

I hope I'm doing right, Lieutenant Gilbert McAllister fretted as he trudged the dusty mile from Fort Creel to Avalanche. He was a big man with huge shoulders that strained the seams of his sweat-damp cavalry blouse, and there was no hint of softness in his bulk. But what he carried in the buckskin bag clutched in his thick-muscled fist weighed heavy on him. And as he reached the flat adobe town the doubt kept nagging at him: I sure hope this is the right thing to do.

He strode past the wood-frame warehouse with the afternoon sun scorching his shoulders, and climbed up into the shade of the boardwalk where the express office sided the two-story adobe hotel. His boots scraped on the walk. He wiped his wet right palm against his yellow-striped cavalry trousers, shifted the buckskin bag from his left hand to his right, and wiped his left palm on his other trouser leg. He was perspiring profusely as he reached the town corral. Trickles of moisture ran down over the chinstrap that anchored his campaign hat in place.

McAllister was usually as sure of himself as a man could be. He'd become an officer the hardest way there was: by making the astronomical leap over the barrier from sergeant to lieutenant two years back, when he was thirty. That gave a man confidence in his own decisions. But now his beefy red face was uncertain.

He glanced over the horses in the corral, turned on his heel and stalked into the stable.

Potter, the weedy little stableman, greeted him. "Hi, Lieutenant. Lookin' to buy a good mount?"

McAllister shook his head. "That fellow who brought Mrs. Graff back—he put his horse up here?"

"Uh-huh. You want my opinion of what Graff oughta do with that Injun-lovin' wife of his?"

"I don't," McAllister snapped. "What's the name of the fellow who brought her in?"

"Didn't say. Tall, skinny man."

"Where's his horse?"

Potter nodded at one of the stalls at the rear of the stable. "He's sure gaunted up some. Carrying double all that way. Drank a tankful of water and enough good feed to bust a gut."

McAllister strode back to the stall. The horse in it was a coyote dun, with black mane, hoof and tail, and a dark streak along its back. McAllister recognized the horse. Lobo. Jess had borrowed from him to buy this horse.

McAllister left the stable and walked down the boardwalk to the entrance of the hotel. As he hesitated there, he saw Jess Remsberg emerge from the restaurant down the block and pause at the hitch-rail to roll and light a cigarette. His faded Levis, denim jacket and shapeless Stetson were streaked with sweat and caked with dust. His boots were old and in sorry condition, one of them stitched up the side where the leather had torn.

Jess Remsberg was as tall as McAllister, but compared to the lieutenant's big slab of a body, Jess looked like a shadow. He'd always been lean as a whip, but to McAllister he now looked thinner than he'd ever been.

Jess dragged deep at his cigarette, blew out a stream of gray smoke, and limped across the dry dirt street to the adobe saloon. McAllister remembered how Jess had acquired that limp: an arrow in the hip in the Ojo Caliente fight with Victorio's warriors. McAllister had a vivid image of himself down with a bullet in his chest, watching Jess crawl toward him with blood streaming down the shaft of that arrow. Jess had dragged him behind the rocks before passing out on top of him.

Gil McAllister sighed heavily. He looked up at the black clouds gathering on the horizon, at the barracks roofs of Fort Creel a mile off, and at the distant Arizona hills hanging in the haze. He looked down at the small buckskin bag in his big hand, and the muscles of his face hardened. He crossed the street and strode toward the adobe saloon, his heavy legs carrying him almost against his will.

It took a few seconds for his eyes to adjust to the cool gloom inside the long, narrow room. A few men were at the bar, the manager of the express office, a couple of miners, and a professional gambler named Toller. Jess was alone at a table, with a bottle and a glass. He was drinking the stuff as if it were water.

"Hello, Jess. Thirsty?"

Jess looked up quickly. When he saw McAllister, the hard shine went out of his gray eyes. His wide mouth fashioned a smile that made McAllister heartsick; he remembered when Jess used to grin as if he meant it.

"Gil," Jess said, "I must've swallowed a ton of dust. Can't wash it down."

McAllister dropped heavily onto a chair opposite Jess. He put the buckskin bag on the table. Jess glanced at it curiously, then at the officer's troubled face.

"Here." Jess pushed the bottle and glass across the table.

McAllister started to shake his head, but changed his mind. Ignoring the glass, he seized the bottle and put it to his mouth, tilting it and swallowing deep. The raw burn of it made tears spring to his eyes. He put the bottle down with a thump.

"Christ!" he gasped. "What're you drinking these days?"

"Not the best, I admit. Just the best a poor vaquero can afford. I was going to come over to the fort to see you soon as I washed some of the dry out of me. How'd you know I was here?"

"Word came over that somebody had brought Mrs. Graff back. They said the man was skinny as a straw and ugly as sin, so I figured it might be you."

Jess barely managed a smile at that. "Gil," he asked, "what's the story on Ellen Graff?"

McAllister shook his head slowly. "Complicated. She got took by a band of Chata's Apaches almost two years ago, when they were raiding east through New Mexico. A couple of months back a cavalry company hit Chata's home base in the Sierra Anchas while Chata and his warriors were out on a raid. They busted up the village pretty bad. Somebody clubbed Mrs. Graff with the stock of a carbine and knocked her out before they spotted her red hair and saw she was white. They took her out with them, brought her here to her husband."

"I met her husband," Jess commented dryly. "He didn't seem anxious to get her back this time."

McAllister looked down at his big hands. "Well, it's a sorry story for sure, Jess. You know the Chiricahuas have only one use for a white woman. Only reason they didn't kill her when they were finished with her was that Chata's oldest son, Nachee, took a fancy to her on account of her red hair. Made her quite a curiosity, that hair. They called her Flame because of its color. Nachee bought her for one of his wives. Guess Graff didn't like getting back an Apache's leavings."

"He's a fool," Jess said tonelessly. The strange bond he'd felt between himself and Ellen Graff drew tighter. This was a land of war between the Indian and the white man, and Jess and Ellen Graff had gotten themselves caught in the middle of it.

McAllister said, "We're all fools, one way or another, Jess. What makes it more complicated is that it turns out Mrs. Graff had a son by Nachee. The boy got left behind when the cavalry pulled out of Chata's camp. Graff said she threatened to go back to hunt for the boy. Nobody took her serious till she disappeared with one of Graff's horses one night a couple of weeks back. Guess she was looking for Chata's band when you found her. A sorry story."

Jess nodded, staring at the bottle. He picked it up, and drank from it the way McAllister had, only he drank more, and he didn't strangle on it. When he set the bottle down, it was half empty. McAllister couldn't remember Jess ever drinking like that. Jess's eyes looked glazed when he set the bottle down, as though the raw whisky had stunned his brain.

Jess wiped his wet mouth with the dusty sleeve of his denim jacket and looked up to meet McAllister's eyes. "I wasn't sure you'd still be here, Gil. I figured you might be gone by now."

"It took me longer to get up here than I thought it would when I sent you that telegram from Fort Duell. Coming up here from Duell was five hundred miles of pure hell."

Jess nodded. "I thought things had tamed down some."

McAllister shook his head. "Getting bad again. Chata got away from us last time. He's down in Mexico now, somewhere in the Tres Castillos Mountains."

"I heard he didn't have much of a band left after the cavalry caught him last time."

"That's right. But he's still alive. And Apaches have been sneaking off the reservation by the dozen and slipping down across the border to join him, slaughtering anybody they run across on the way. The army's scared that when Chata builds his band up again, he'll come north of the border. Then we'll have another thing on our hands like Victorio, or Nana's raid."

"That why you're here?"

"Yeah. If Chata comes across, the main operation against him will have to be out of Fort Duell in the south. I'm here to take an ammunition train and more troops down to Duell. If he gets past us down there, no American or Mexican in Arizona, New Mexico or Texas will be safe."

"That's so," Jess agreed. "If he isn't caught when he comes across the border, he won't ever be caught. Not till he's done a hell of a lot of damage, anyway."

"Remember Tom Van?" McAllister asked.

Jess's eyes clouded. He nodded.

"Tom came up with me from Duell. After I got here I

sent him out to see if he could follow some of the Apaches heading down to join Chata. He's going to try to check on Chata's force, find out if he's getting strong enough to raid north soon."

Jess placed his hands flat on the table and squinted at the big officer. "Tom Van's dead," he told McAllister. "I found him staked out less than sixty miles from here."

McAllister's face froze with shock. After a minute of absorbing it, he licked his lips and muttered: "I never figured any Indian could get Tom Van."

"They got him," Jess stated flatly.

"That's bad. Real bad. I'll have to send a report to . . ." McAllister grabbed up the bottle, hesitated, then set it down again without drinking from it. He watched Jess pick up the bottle immediately and drink slowly. The hard planes of Jess's face were going slack from the liquor.

McAllister's eyes wandered to the small buckskin bag. "I didn't know if you'd show up here, Jess. Heard you were working for a ranch in California, but that was a couple of months back. I sent the telegram just on the chance you'd still be there, not knowing if you'd get it."

"I got it. Came part of the way on mule back, so it was late getting to me. Telegram said you had to see me real urgent. What about, Gil?"

McAllister veiled his eyes and squinted down at his huge fists on the table. "Thought maybe you'd have moved on by this time," he said, skirting the subject nervously.

Jess said quietly, "I got no place to go."

"You've been going a lot of places in the last year, Jess."

"Not any more. I stopped looking."

McAllister felt the doubt within him building up. "You really gave up?"

"Not much sense to it. I know I'm not going to find whoever did it. Should have known that from the start. The only hope was that whoever he was he'd do some talking about it, and maybe I'd hear something. But it's too big a country, Gil. Awful big."

"If you've given it up, why didn't you come back?"

"What for?"

"Army needs good scouts as bad as ever."

Jess picked up the empty glass and rolled it back and forth between his lean hands, studying it. "Tell you the truth, Gil," he said at last, "I don't have the guts for it any more."

"I don't believe that, Jess."

"It's so. Not any more. When I quit hunting whoever did it . . . When I finally got it through my thick skull that I was just running around the country blind like a chicken with its head cut off . . . Well, something sort of drained out of me."

When he looked up at McAllister, there was pain in his gray eyes. "I don't want to come back, Gil. If that's why you sent me that telegram, forget it. I have a job. I don't give a damn about any troubles anybody else has, including the army."

"It's been a year, Jess. That's a long time to mourn."

Jess looked surprised. "I'm not mourning. Been a long time since I did any mourning. I don't even hate anymore. It's as if it happened to somebody else."

McAllister saw that Jess was well on his way to getting drunk—and that Jess's hands were trembling on the table.

"Somebody else," Jess went on in a voice low and strained. "So why should I give a damn? I don't. Not any more."

McAllister's fingers quivered as they seized the small buckskin bag. "I don't know if this is the right thing to do," he said. "I just don't know, Jess."

Jess stared at the bag with blank eyes. His mouth was open. He seemed to be bracing himself, as though he already knew.

McAllister opened the strings and gently took out what was inside. He placed it carefully on the table.

It was a scalp. Oil had been used on it to preserve it. The hair was black and long, formed in two thick braids—the hair of an Indian woman.

A white streak ran through the hair for a few inches at the

front. Bits of blue flannel had been worked into the braids. One tiny silver bell hung from a strip of the blue flannel on each braid.

Jess stared down at it for a long time. Slowly, his hands crawled across the table to it. His trembling fingers gently stroked the smooth black hair. His body was wracked by terrible, soundless sobs.

The flesh of McAllister's back crawled. He looked at Jess and saw that his eyes were empty. Empty of tears, or anything else. McAllister felt his own eyes getting hot and misty.

"Jess," he said, "I wasn't sure it was hers. But that white streak . . . when I saw that I remembered. It always looked so pretty. Her so young, and that white . . ."

Jess drew the scalp close to him on the table, his hands caressing the braids, his face like that of a man newly blinded.

McAllister shuddered. He talked to stave off dizziness. "The sutler at Fort Duell had it up on his wall for show. Said he bought it from the town marshal. The marshal's new, a man named Clay Dean. From up in north Texas. Since that's where it happened I felt pretty sure . . . I went to look for him, but he was away somewhere. I got sent here before he got back, so I sent that telegram." McAllister pulled a checked handkerchief from his pocket and mopped his face. "I hope I'm doing the right thing, Jess. All the time I kept worrying whether I was making a mistake, getting in touch with you about it. But I got to thinking you wouldn't ever pull yourself together, until . . ."

Jess flicked the tiny silver bell on one of the braids with his forefinger. "I took these off a Christmas tree for her," he whispered.

One of the men at the bar had come over to the table, was looking down at what was in Jess's hands. It was Toller, the gambler.

"That's a mighty interesting scalp you've got there,"

Toller remarked in a friendly way. McAllister and Jess looked up at him.

Toller looked at McAllister. If he'd looked at Jess and seen his expression, he might not have gone on the way he did: "I know where an Injun scalp like that would bring a pretty good price. How much do you want for it?"

Jess let go of the hair and stood up slowly, staring at Toller. His mouth hung open. There was insanity in his face.

McAllister lunged to his feet and swung on Jess with a short, chopping motion of his right arm. His clenched fist made a sound like a rock slamming against the side of Jess's head at the temple.

McAllister caught him as he fell, and lowered him gently to the floor. He turned back to the table, scooped up the scalp, and carefully enclosed it in the buckskin bag.

Toller looked from the man on the floor to the big cavalry officer, his face blank with surprise. "What did you do that for?"

McAllister hitched the buckskin bag under the waistband of his trousers, under his cavalry blouse. He looked at the shocked Toller. "I just saved your life," McAllister told him. "He was going to kill you."

"What for? All I did was ask the price of an Injun's scalp."

McAllister bent over, grabbed the unconscious Jess, and lifted him easily in his powerful arms.

"Yeah," McAllister said as he straightened with his burden. "Only it happens to be his wife's scalp."

He went out into the blazing sunlight and began the mile hike back to the fort, carrying Jess in his arms.

THREE

Jess came awake on the hard bunk in McAllister's tiny room at the army post. He opened his eyes slowly and stared up at the log beams slashed with streaks of sunlight that came through the strings of beads curtaining the room's single small window. It was stifling hot in the room. Jess went on staring up at the beams until memory came back to him. He remembered up to the moment the gambler came to the table and made his offer for Singing Sky's hair. After that his memory came against a blank.

Jess turned his head to look for McAllister. The motion caught the spine of his neck in a clamp of agony. Something popped in his brain like a firecracker. He squeezed his eyes shut against the pain. When the firecracker burned itself out against the top of his skull, he carefully opened his eyes again. McAllister's broad blue-uniformed back was to him. He was pouring something into a glass on the desk.

McAllister turned to him with the glass. "Here. Drink this, Jess."

Jess started to shake his head, stopped himself in time. "No. No more whiskey."

"This is water, with something in it for your head. Got it from the post surgeon."

McAllister slipped a thick arm under Jess's shoulders and raised him a bit. Lifting his hands to take the glass started twinges like fish hooks digging into the nerves between Jess's shoulder blades. He kept his head bent to one side,

21

afraid to try straightening it. It was hard to swallow. He had
to force the liquid down in slow gulps. He couldn't taste it at
all.

McAllister took the glass away from him and let him lean
back again.

"What happened?" Jess croaked.

"I hit you," McAllister told him.

Jess thought back for a moment. "Good thing you did."

He watched McAllister set the glass on the desk. His
head was beginning to swim. His stomach felt as if it was
rising against his lungs. He swallowed hard and whispered:
"Where is it, Gil?"

McAllister took the small buckskin bag from under his
military blouse and passed it over. Jess held it with both
hands on his chest for a moment. Then he opened the
drawstrings and reached slowly inside with one hand. His
fingers touched the smooth hair in the bag, caressing the
braids gently.

One of the tiny bells tinkled. Jess began to cry then, the
tears coming without sound, without any change in his
numbed face. The tears blinded him, and the swimming in
his brain engulfed him. He felt himself slide easily back into
darkness.

When he awoke again, the sunlight had gone from the
ceiling beams. There was a dull, persistent ache in the side
of his head where McAllister had slugged him, but he found
he could turn his stiff neck without starting any fireworks.
The light outside the bead curtain was graying into dusk.
The room itself was dim except for a circle of yellow
thrown out by the harp lamp on the desk where McAllister
sat studying a spread-out map.

Jess became conscious of the thick braid of hair clutched
tightly in his right hand. Without looking down, he
loosened his fist and withdrew his hand from the bag. He
closed the drawstrings, got his elbows under him, and sat
up. He felt surprisingly clearheaded and empty of emotion.
When he swung his legs off the side of the bunk and set his
feet on the floor, McAllister looked up quickly from his

map. The lamplight shone on McAllister's wide jaw and firm mouth, but left the upper part of his face in gloom.

"How do you feel, Jess?"

"Pretty fair." Jess rubbed his face with his tough palms.

"Hungry?"

"No. What are you up to?"

"Picking the quickest route back to Fort Duell."

"Better to pick a careful one."

"No need to. I'll have twenty-five troopers with the ammunition train. There's nothing out there but stray Apaches heading down from the reservation. Nothing for a cavalry troop to worry about until Chata comes north out of Mexico."

"How do you know he hasn't, already?"

"If he had, we'd have heard. When he does come across the border, he'll let us know he's back awful fast."

The two men sat in silence for a while, looking at each other through the deepening gloom. McAllister turned up the lamp to have a better look at Jess. The tall, thin man sat on the edge of the bunk cradling the closed buckskin bag in both hands on his lap. Despite the big bruise at his temple and the dark patches under his wide eyes, something about Jess had improved. There was a new strength and certainty to him, as though everything inside him had at last come back into focus.

"What are you going to do, Jess?" McAllister asked him.

"You told me who you got her hair from."

"The sutler at Duell." McAllister nodded. "But he isn't the man who raped and killed your wife, Jess. I'm sure of that. He bought her scalp from the new town marshal, Clay Dean."

"Then you know what I'm going to do, Gil. I'm going to Fort Duell after this Clay Dean." There was no emotion in Jess Remsberg's voice now. He spoke with a quiet calm that made McAllister shiver.

"You know how he's going to die, Gil? Slow. The way

the Chiricahuas would do it. I'll keep him alive for days . . . ''

McAllister's mouth was suddenly very dry. "Jess," he said, "Clay Dean may not be the one. He may have bought her scalp, the way the sutler did."

"If that's so, he'll tell me. I'll talk to him and he'll tell me who he bought her hair from. I never had any kind of trail to follow before. Now it's there, waiting for me. All I have to do is keep going until I reach the man who killed her."

McAllister wiped the sweat from his sunburned cheeks with his sleeve. "Jess," he said, "I know that whoever did it has to die. That's why I sent you the telegram. It's right he should die, but not the way you're planning to do it. You do it the way you say you will, and you won't ever be the same again. It'll dirty you for the rest of your life. Just kill him quick and clean."

Jess shook his head slowly, and McAllister was horrified to see that he was smiling. "What happened was partly my fault, I guess," Jess said. "Maybe I'm to blame because I took a Comanche girl for my bride. I'm the one that was stupid enough to take her with me to where there was war with Apaches and everybody hated any kind of Indian. But if it's partly my fault, I've paid for it."

"It's wrong to blame yourself for anything, Jess."

"No. The man that caught her alone and took her hair is going to pay," Jess went on, not listening. "It's his turn to pay. And not just by dying. That'll only be the end of his paying, and he'll be praying for it, screaming for it, when it comes."

McAllister's eyes narrowed on his friend, and his face grew hard. "Leave off that kind of talk, Jess. That kind of thing is what comes out of blood-mad Apaches. No civilized white man can stomach it, let alone do it himself."

"It was no Apache that killed Singing Sky and took her hair. That was one of your civilized white men."

"A white man," McAllister conceded. "But not civilized. Not any more. Not when he did that to her. We're fighting a war with savages, Jess. We've got to tame 'em, and to kill the ones that won't be tamed. Maybe some day whoever's left of them will learn civilization from us, and then they won't be savages any more." McAllister didn't take his eyes from Jess as he spoke. "But for some white men it's just the opposite. Fighting savages, they lose the civilization in them and become savages too, like the one who killed Singing Sky. When that happens, they've got to be exterminated just like the rest of the savages we're fighting—the way you'll have to be exterminated, Jess, if you've become contaminated too."

Jess stood up and went to the desk, took the saucer off the top of the pitcher that sat here. He poured water from it into the glass and gulped it all down. Then he poured the glass full again and drained that off too.

"I got a terrible dry in me, Gil. Seems as if I can drink till my gut swells and I'm still thirsty."

McAllister saw that he had closed the subject and would not reopen it. "Jess, I'll be heading for Duell in a couple of days with the ammunition train. You can go along with us."

Jess shook his head. "Too slow. I'm starting out tonight."

"That's bad country to travel alone in, Jess. You might not make it to Duell that way. You want whoever did it to outlive you? Better go with me, slowly, and make it there."

Jess looked down at the perspiring McAllister and grinned without mirth. "You just want to be with me when I get him. You figure I'll let him die quick and easy if you're there."

McAllister nodded. "That's partly it," he admitted. "But I can use you as a scout on the way, too. I was figuring Tom Van would be back. But you're just as good."

"No," Jess said.

"You owe me a favor," McAllister snapped. "I didn't have to send you that telegram. I could have left you to drink yourself to death never knowing. So you owe me this when I ask it of you."

Uncertainty twisted Jess's features. "You don't really need me to scout for you."

"Yes, I do." McAllister planted his thick forearms on the spread-out map and met Jess's eyes firmly. "I've already made one mistake in sending Tom Van out to be killed. I don't want anything more to go wrong. I want to deliver twenty-five fresh troopers and that load of ammunition intact to Duell."

He grinned suddenly at Jess. "I can't afford any mistakes on my record. I'm going to get to be a general some day."

"It's a long way up from sergeant to general."

"I'm a lieutenant now, I'll make it. Look at Bernard. He moved up from sergeant to officer rank. The last I heard he's sure to be made brigadier general soon."

"Didn't remember you being so damn ambitious, Gil."

"I didn't have a reason to be. Now I do. I'm going to get married, Jess. Remember Sergeant Nimier's daughter?"

"Sarah Nimier." Jess's memory went back to a golden-haired little girl with big eyes and a quick laugh. "I remember her. Congratulations, Gil."

"I want to live to have kids, Jess. And I want them to grow up proud of me. I want you to scout for me on the way back to Duell. I'll take it bad if you turn me down."

Jess shrugged. "I guess a week more or less won't change anything. I'll go with you."

McAllister flattened his big hands hard on the desk top to hide their sudden trembling. "Good. Why don't you go get some food into you? You need it, even if you don't feel hungry."

"I'm going back to town to get Lobo and my things first." Jess carefully slipped the small buckskin bag under the belt of his Levis. "I'll get something to eat in town."

Jess started for the door. McAllister's voice stopped him: "Jess!"

Jess turned back. "Yeah?"

McAllister cleared his throat nervously. "We ought to bury Singing Sky's hair, Jess. It isn't right for it not to be buried like the rest of her."

"I'll bury it," Jess said softly. "But not yet. After I get the man that took it off her—then I'll bury the rest of her."

* * *

Jess went down off the boardwalk onto the dusty parade ground and crossed it to the gate. Leaving the post behind, he strode slowly toward the town through the gathering gloom of dusk. While his long legs ate up the distance, his mind soared far from this place and time—darted to the young face of his Comanche bride, to her corpse lying beside the stream the way he'd found it, to a faceless man somewhere in the vicinity of Fort Duell. . . .

It was almost dark when he reached the town; lights were beginning to show in windows. As he limped past the adobe house beside the frame warehouse, he saw the light of a lamp go on inside.

He hesitated for a moment, then went on toward the stable. His thoughts were suddenly of Ellen Graff. He thought of the name the Apaches had given her: Flame.

Inside the kitchen, Ellen Graff ladled stew from the steaming pot on the woodstove onto two plates. She carried the plates into the main room, where her husband sat with his elbows on the table, staring blankly at the painting of a storm-tossed ocean that hung on the wall. The bruise on his cheekbone under his left eye was swelling and turning black.

Ellen set one plate in front of him, the other in front of the other chair across the table from him.

"I'm not hungry," he said without looking at her.

She went back into the kitchen and stood there beside the stove for a few moments, stiffly, biting her lower lip. A strand of dark red hair slipped down on her forehead, over the white scar where the carbine stock had struck her when the cavalry had smashed into Chata's camp. She pushed the strand of red hair back into place with a swift movement of her hand. She took up the bread and the butter dish and went back into the main room.

When she was seated across from her husband, she looked at the bruise under his eye.

"Millard," she said softly, "you don't have to fight because of me. There's no use to it."

He raised his head and looked at her, his face dark with anger. "You think I can let a man say something insulting about you and still hold my head up?" He looked at his skinned knuckles and grimaced, moving his burly shoulders to loosen the tension of their muscles. "That's one miner better get a strike. He'll need a lot of gold to make himself new teeth."

He looked down at his plate and pushed it away from him irritably. "I told you I wasn't hungry."

"You have to eat, Millard."

"Why?" There was a whine of self-pity in his voice, the look of it softening his handsome face. "You don't know how many times I've had to fight because of you. Not so much any more, because they know what I'll do if they say anything in my hearing!"

"I'm sorry, Millard," Ellen said tonelessly. "Sorry they brought me back to ruin your life." Bitterness stiffened her face.

But her husband wasn't looking at her. He was looking at his clenched fists. "I'm making out okay now, getting bigger in these parts. I was on my way to bein' an important man in this place. But now . . . Most feel sorry for me, pity me. I know it. But some of them think it's a big joke. Very funny—my wife comes back after she's bedded with a whole tribe of bucks and had a kid by one of them."

The white scar on Ellen Graff's forehead went livid. "I didn't do it because I wanted to!" she screamed at him. "I had to! You know that! Talk about pity! Have you none for me?"

His eyes clouded with confusion and shame. "I have, Ellen," he mumbled. "I swear I have. But it's hard. Don't you see how I feel? My God, you were even a wife to one of them."

"Not because I wanted to be."

"Then why were you? Other women've been grabbed by Indians. Any decent white woman would kill herself before she'd let . . ."

"I'm not that decent, I guess, or that brave. I was afraid to die. I still am. Even now."

Graff, angry at finding himself suddenly on the defensive, lashed back at her: "That's all it was? You were afraid they'd kill you? Is that why you run off again, just a couple days back, to go back to them instead of being safe here?"

"My son is with them. He's all I have. I want my son."

"Your son! You call a thing fathered by an Apache your son? God, I was right! You got no decency left in you."

Ellen Graff looked down at her untouched food, her face hard, and did not speak.

"You think they'd have let you just pick up that kid and go off with him?" Millard Graff went on. "They'd have kept you there, don't you know that? I guess you do. Maybe you figure that's where you belong now, living with a bunch of savages."

"I don't belong anywhere," she said without looking up. "I don't belong here any more. I belong only to my son now."

"Stop calling that thing your son!"

Ellen Graff looked up then, and her green eyes were bright and fierce. "He is my son. Mine. His hair is red, like mine. He looks like me."

Disgust twisted Millard Graff's features into something ugly. "I *am* sorry for you," he rasped harshly. "You're not normal any more. It's not your fault. I guess they drove you crazy."

Ellen stared down at her plate. After a moment, mechanically, she picked up a fork. And then she began to sob wildly.

Millard Graff watched her cry, and confusion tore at his emotions again. When her sobbing got worse, a horrible, choking thing that went on out of control, he cried out: "Stop it, Ellen! Stop it!"

It went on, and he wanted to touch her but couldn't bring himself to.

"Ellen, please! You think I'm rotten? Well, so do I. But I'm all mixed up. I don't know what to . . . My God,

Ellen, if you'd seen me after I found out those Apaches had taken you! I went pure crazy for a while. For months I tried to find them, to find you. And then I finally got it into my head that you must be dead. That they must have killed you. I had to start a new life for myself. Didn't I have to do that, Ellen? Wouldn't . . ."

Ellen Graff suddenly wrenched herself up out of her chair and ran out of the room into the kitchen. He sat and watched the door slam shut behind her, heard the door at the rear of the house slam a moment later.

He put his elbows on the table and buried his face wearily in his hands. The fabric of his life was torn now, and nothing could mend it. His ambitions were useless. The future for which he'd worked so hard the past five years was a vanished mirage, because Ellen had come back from the dead. She was a curse that would hang around his neck for the rest of her life.

Only strangers dared to try hinting things about her within his hearing now, but he knew what everyone else thought about when they looked at him or saw Ellen. He had no chance now of building himself into an important man with people laughing behind his back.

And his hope of marrying Mary Harrap, whose father owned the big Santos mine—that was dead, too.

He felt nothing for Ellen now but revulsion. He couldn't look at her without his mind conjuring up vivid images of her pale body with the dark ones of naked Indians. He couldn't touch her; hadn't touched her since the troopers had brought her back to him.

God knows he had loved her once. It was for her that he'd settled down, taken up freighting, started building for a solid future for the family that was to come. And when she had been seized by those raiding Apaches, his grief had been a scalding wound inside him.

Millard Graff thought back to the months he'd spent frantically searching for her, trying to find the Apache raiders who had taken her, until he'd finally been sure she was dead. And then hate had filled him, replacing the worn-out grief—hatred of all Indians, and a wild lust for revenge. He remembered the two young Apaches he'd ambushed near the Rio Grande, his rifle bullets smashing through their skulls to spatter their brains on the sand. He remembered the old Indian outside the San Carlos reservation who had died painfully under his rage-directed knife work. Both times he'd taken scalps, the way he'd been sure some Apache had taken Ellen's.

He remembered that pretty Indian girl beside the stream in northern Texas. . . .

Millard Graff stared at the door that Ellen had slammed shut when she ran out. That was one thing you had to hand Indian women. They didn't cry like that, no matter what you did to them. That pretty Indian girl he'd taken in an uncontrollable outpouring of hate and lust hadn't cried. She'd fought him, with her eyes dry and hard and savage.

He remembered staring down at that strange little white streak in her glossy black hair before he took her scalp, and those tiny silver bells on her black braids.

FOUR

Jess Remsberg checked on Lobo. The horse, though still gaunted, looked rested and ready to travel. Jess told the stableman he'd settle the bill when he came back for Lobo in an hour or so. Then he left the stable and strolled down the dark street to the lights of the adobe restaurant, walking with a long, loose stride in spite of his limp. The wound that had caused the limp had ceased to pain him long ago, unless he had to move fast or shift position suddenly—then it slowed him up some.

The restaurant was small and dimly lit. The waiter and the bartender were Mexican, and so was the food. Jess sat himself at a scarred wooden table near one end of the bar and told the waiter to bring him whatever they were serving fresh that night. When the bartender asked if he wanted something to drink, Jess shook his head. But the hot Mexican food burned his tongue and the roof of his mouth, so he changed his mind after a few forkfuls and ordered a glass of beer. It wasn't cold, but it helped.

Jess had the fork halfway to his mouth when Toller, the professional gambler, came in. He strode to the bar without seeing Jess and ordered a drink. Jess's eyes followed Toller, though his head didn't move. As Toller tossed off his drink, Jess raised his fork the rest of the way to his mouth. But this time he didn't feel the burn of the peppers mixed with the beans.

Toller ordered another drink. He picked it up and turned

till his back was to the bar, his elbows back against it. Then he saw Jess. Toller, his face expressionless, set the drink back on the bar, untasted. His right hand came back to rest on the buckle of his belt, a motion by which his elbow at the same time pushed back his knee-length black coat to reveal the gun in the holster tied down to his thigh.

He seemed to hesitate a moment. Then he slowly came over to Jess's table. He stopped in front of Jess, looking down at him blankly with dull, dark-brown eyes. His right hand remained on his belt buckle, the gun exposed.

"Your friend said you wanted to kill me," Toller said quietly. Like his face, his voice held no expression.

Jess tried to place the flavor of the gambler's accent. South Carolina, maybe, or someplace near there. Wherever he was from, there was education in Toller's background. But Jess was more sharply aware of the weight of his own holstered gun at the moment, and of his feeling that he wouldn't stand a chance against Toller's draw this close up. He met Toller's eyes and said nothing.

After waiting a moment for Jess to speak, Toller said, "I don't like the idea of someone around town nurturing a desire to kill me. I'd rather settle it now, if that thought is still on your mind."

"It's not."

Something about Toller relaxed abruptly, though his face did not change. "Then I apologize," he said in the same expressionless voice. "I apologize, and sincerely."

Jess was surprised. "No need. You didn't know."

A flicker of something like pain crossed Toller's dark eyes. His right hand moved from his belt buckle to the back of a chair. Jess tried to judge the gambler's age, but dissipation had ruined his face to the point where it was impossible to tell. He might have been anywhere from thirty to fifty. Only his eyes revealed that the ruin had not yet reached his nerves.

"This is a country," Toller said tonelessly, "that makes it difficult for a man to retain decency. If I could have seen myself five years ago, offering to buy and sell an Indian

scalp for profit—a woman's scalp at that—I'd have put a
bullet through my brain. Now I just . . . Would you care
to share a drink with me?"

Jess shook his head. "I've had enough to suit me for a
while."

At that moment their attention was diverted by the noisy
entrance into the restaurant of three blue-uniformed cavalry
troopers. Their boot heels rapped against the hard clay floor
as they shoved up to the bar and shouted their orders. The
one that wore sergeant's stripes on his sleeve glanced over at
Jess and Toller. He was a plump man in his late thirties.
Large, china-blue eyes gazed out of his sunburned plump
face with the innocence of a baby. Few men were fooled by
his appearance. The army didn't make sergeants out of
innocent baby adults—not in Indian country.

The sergeant looked at Jess, his rusty eyebrows going up
a bit. Then he strode down the bar to the table. "Jess
Remsberg!" His voice had a hard snap to it. "You back
with the army?"

Jess nodded, puzzled. He couldn't place the sergeant in
his memory, though he looked familiar.

"You don't know me," the sergeant said. "I was a
private last time you scouted for my troop. You took off
about a week after I joined up." He extended his hand.
"Phil Ferguson."

Jess shook Ferguson's hand. "Now I remember you."

"You scouting for us on the way back to Duell?"

"Yeah."

"Good thing. I hear you found Tom Van dead."

Jess nodded. He forked some more beans into his mouth
and chewed slowly, keeping his mind from the last he'd
seen of Tom Van.

"Van was plenty smart," Sergeant Ferguson said. "I
never figured the Apaches could get him."

Toller cleared his throat and said, "Sergeant, when is
your troop moving back to Fort Duell?"

Sergeant Ferguson's blue eyes lost their friendliness when
he looked at the gambler. "Couple days. Why?"

"I'd like to go along."

"Why?"

"Pickings are getting a bit thin, here," Toller stated frankly. "Hasn't been any traffic in or out of Duell for some time. I imagine the pay money is burning holes in your pockets back there."

"That's a fact," Sergeant Ferguson said.

"So what are my chances of accompanying the troop back to Duell?"

Ferguson shrugged. "It ain't my say. Go ask Lieutenant McAllister. Maybe he'll say you can come along. He's already given permission to Millard Graff."

Jess Remsberg lowered his fork. "Graff?"

"Yeah," Ferguson said. "Graff's a freighter. He figures the same as Toller, here. Fort Duell area's been shut off from freighters for a month because of the Apache trouble. Graff knows he can sell a wagonload of goods for big profit there. He's right, too. My wife needs cloth for a new dress real bad."

Toller said, "If Graff is allowed this opportunity for a strong escort to Fort Duell, I don't see how I can be denied the same thing. I have the same civilian rights to army protection."

"Like I said," Ferguson told him, "it ain't up to me."

"McAllister in town?"

"No. Over at the fort."

Toller nodded to Jess. "We may be companions on the journey, Mr. Remsberg." He hurried out of the restaurant.

Jess stared after him, thinking of Millard Graff's going to Fort Duell, leaving his wife here alone. He rose to his feet, paid for his meal at the bar. "See you later," he said to Sergeant Ferguson, and went out toward the stable.

The stableman wasn't inside. Jess went to Lobo's stall. The coyote dun horse whinnied at his approach and toed the ground. Jess patted Lobo's sleek neck and looked around for his saddle.

A woman screamed in the corral behind the stable.

Ice shivered up Jess's spine; shock froze him there for a

second. Then he hurried through the stable toward the door
at the rear.

Outside the rear of the stable a lighted lantern hung
beside the door. Its meager gleam fell upon the figures of
four people in the corral, between the tethered horses and
the stable. Three of them were men: the stableman and two
miners from the nearby hills. The miners looked like
brothers; dressed alike, both short, thick-bodied, black-
bearded.

One of the miners had hold of a woman: Ellen Graff. Her
face was twisted with terror. Her red hair fell forward over
her eyes as the miner holding her by her arms shook her
back and forth brutally.

Jess stopped in the shadow just outside the stable door
and stared from one to the other. The hate he carried inside
him swelled abruptly. The thin wall he'd learned to erect
around that hate began to crack apart.

"Let her go," he said softly. His booted legs spread
slightly apart in the dust of the corral. He leaned forward a
bit, balanced.

The heads of the three men jerked around toward him.
The one holding Ellen stopped shaking her. But he didn't let
go of her arms. He snapped, "Like hell I'll let her go! She
tried to steal our horses."

"She should be horsewhipped," the stableman growled.
"And thrown into jail."

"Naw," said the other miner. There was drunkenness in
his voice. "We'll let her go . . . if she'll be nice to us like
she been to all them Apache bucks. What' d'ya say, lady?"

"Let her go," Jess rasped. He took a step toward them.
The stableman backed off in a hurry.

"Sure!" yelled the miner holding Ellen. He flung her
away from him, sending her sprawling in the dust of the
corral. The next instant he was leaping at Jess, his meaty fist
swinging.

Jess stopped thinking, his instincts taking over. The
muscles of his middle jerked tight as he threw up his hands
and caught the blow on his forearm. His boot shot out and

up, its heel sinking into the miner's stomach. The man
folded like a snapped stick. Before he hit the ground, the
other miner slammed into Jess, almost knocking him off his
feet.

Their arms went around each other, each trying to
squeeze the breath out of the other. Jess felt the miner's
arms tighten like iron hands, grinding his ribcage, and knew
the other man was stronger than he. He got one foot off the
ground, brought it down hard on the miner's ankle. The man
gasped, and Jess wrenched out of his grip.

The miner's fist slammed against his temple. Jess's head
rocked. He staggered blindly, tripped and fell to the ground
on his back. The miner came down on top of him, his
weight knocking the breath out of Jess's lungs. Jess heaved
his shoulders and brought up his head with a jerk. His
forehead cracked against the miner's nose, caving it flat.
The miner strangled on his blood. But before Jess could
heave him off, the other miner closed in, bent over against
the pain in his middle.

Jess struggled to claw his way upright. He got to his
knees. A boot slammed against his hip, knuckles skidded
over his cheek. Their combined weights bore him back to
the ground. Fingers clawed at his eyes. Jess opened his
mouth and sank his teeth into one of those fingers, through
flesh and muscle to the bone. At the same time he reached
upwards with one free hand and seized an ear with his
steely, thin fingers. Twisting the ear with all his strength, he
jerked his arm to one side. The man whose ear he pulled
went over on his side with a cry. The finger caught between
Jess's teeth ripped out of his mouth, leaving a gush of blood
behind. Jess bucked upward, hurling off the other miner. An
instant later he was up on his feet, free of both of them.

The nearest one was coming up from the ground on his
knees. Jess kicked him in the head, flopping him over on his
back. Before the miner could roll away, Jess leaped into the
air and came down heels-first onto the man's stomach. The
man's scream chopped short. His arms fell limply at his
sides. Jess lost his footing on the unconscious miner's body
and sprawled face-down in the dust beside him.

Before he could rise, the other miner was beside him, aiming a boot at Jess's head. Jess jerked up his arm and took the kick on his shoulder. The force of it threw Jess completely over, agony shooting down his arm and wrenching his spine. He kept rolling rapidly to avoid the miner's next kick. Getting his hands and knees under him, Jess scrambled backward as a third kick swooshed past his ear. He managed to rise to his feet before the miner could close in again.

The miner checked his rush when he saw Jess up and ready to meet it. Instead, he moved in slowly, crouching. Jess saw that he was the miner whose nose he'd crushed. There was blood matting the lower half of his face. Jess saw something else, just as the miner got in close and sprang: the wicked gleam of a knife in the man's right hand, its point darting up at Jess's middle.

It was too late for Jess to go for his own knife or his gun. As the miner surged against him, the knife springing up, Jess did three things at once as though three separate springs inside him had uncoiled simultaneously. His left hand slapped down against the inside of the miner's right wrist, closing on it and shoving it to one side. His right forearm jerked up under the miner's chin. His right leg shot out behind the miner's ankles and kicked his legs out from under him.

The miner slammed down against the ground on his back. Jess dropped to one knee, the other coming up under the man's right elbow. His left hand retaining its grip on the wrist, he slapped his right down on the miner's bicep. Jess's shoulders hunched forward, exerting an abrupt surge of pressure downward on the arm that was caught across his knee. The miner's elbow broke with a sickening snap.

Jess stood up and kicked away the knife that had fallen from the miner's strengthless hand. Jess stood there for a moment, his chest heaving, dragging in great gulps of air that burned his lungs. The miner did not get up. He sat in the dust holding his destroyed arm, moaning and cursing, his dazed eyes staring at the unconscious, sprawled figure of his brother ten yards away.

Jess turned suddenly to face the stableman, who was backed up against the rear of the stable.

"Not me!" the stableman blurted. "I didn't lay a finger on you! I wasn't going to do anything to her—just tell her husband, is all."

There was a pounding in Jess's ears, a hot pressure against the back of his eyes. Feeling dizzy, he spread his legs further apart for balance and glanced around the corral. Ellen Graff was gone. Jess turned back to the stableman. He spat blood at the ground, wiped his wet mouth with his sleeve. His front teeth were loose and his whole body ached.

"Don't tell her husband anything," he said to the stableman. It was hard to get the words out against his panting. "Just forget the whole thing."

"Her husband ought to be told," the stableman insisted. "She's got no right to . . ."

"I said forget it!" Jess took a step toward the stableman.

The stableman's hands came up, palms out, to ward him off. "All right! I won't say anything. I swear it!"

Jess walked past him into the stable. Inside, he had to lean against a stall post till the trembling of his legs quieted and strength came back to his knees. It took him longer than usual to saddle and bridle Lobo, and tie on the saddlebags. He led the dun out of his stall and climbed aboard him, rode slowly out of the stable.

Ellen Graff was across the street, sitting on the edge of the boardwalk in front of the general story. The light from the store window cast harsh shadows across her bowed back. She leaned with her arms on her lap, staring down at the dusty street as though she were in a trance, unable to move. Jess reined in and watched her.

A flat-bed wagon drawn by a mule rattled slowly up the street, a farmer at the reins with his wife up beside him. The farmer's wife turned her head to stare down eagerly, maliciously at Ellen Graff. Then she turned and said something to her husband. The farmer stared straight ahead, driving the mule, pretending to be unaware of Ellen Graff and of what his wife was saying to him.

A middle-aged man in good city clothes came down the boardwalk. He stopped when he spotted Ellen Graff, stared at her. She appeared to take no more notice of him than she had of the couple on the wagon. He spat contemptuously at the dust of the street and stalked past her.

Jess nudged Lobo across the street to her.

"Hello, Mrs. Graff."

She looked up slowly, her eyes dull. Her red hair still hung over her forehead. The sullen set of her face destroyed her prettiness.

"So you saved me again, Mr. Remsberg," she said quietly. "This time you saved my honor." Her short, sudden laugh was startling. There was nothing pleasant about it. "Thank you."

It twisted his heart. It had been a long time since he'd felt anything for another person's suffering. But he wasn't surprised by what he felt for her. She was like coming upon someone of his own kind in a world of strangers. What did startle him was the depth of pleasure he got from her presence. He hadn't realized that he was so lonely.

He extended a hand down to her. "Come on up here, Mrs. Graff. I'll ride you out of town aways. Clear your head."

She stared up at him, confused. "Why?"

He found himself grinning at her. "Why not? You like it here? Don't worry. I'll get you back home safe."

She stood up uncertainly.

Jess snapped, "Come on."

There was no resistance in her. She took his hand, got her foot up on the toe of his boot in the stirrup. She came up with his pull, settled sideways in front of him. Jess touched Lobo with his heels and headed up the street.

They left the lights of the town behind and entered the star-filled night. A short way out of town, Jess halted the dun near a mammoth boulder. He eased Ellen down off Lobo and dismounted himself. She stood there, gazing at him in the star-softened darkness. Jess sat on the ground and leaned back against the boulder. After a moment, Ellen lowered herself to the ground beside him.

Jess slowly built himself a cigarette and lighted it, waiting for her to say something. She sat beside him, not touching him with any part of her, and stared off into the darkness, saying nothing.

Jess dragged on his cigarette. When he had it half smoked, he said softly, "You got to give up the idea of going to Chata's band after your kid, Mrs. Graff. The Chiricahuas'll most likely kill you for running away."

"I didn't run away," she muttered, not looking at him. "I was taken away. Unconscious. Obviously, you've been told the whole dirty story."

Jess took another drag at his cigarette, expelled the smoke slowly and watched it rise away from him, a cobweb of gray merging into the velvety blackness. "You've got to find some way to make a new life for yourself," he said.

"You don't know what you're talking about!" she snapped angrily. "There is no life for someone like me to find. Nothing."

Jess looked at his cigarette, flicked it away from him. He tore a spike of bear grass from a clump growing beside the boulder, broke it in his fingers and crushed it between his palms, smelling the sharp, tangy fragrance that rose from his hands.

"Mrs. Graff, I do understand. We're alike in something, you see. We've both got ourselves caught in the middle of a war that's going on all the time out here."

She looked at him then, not getting what he meant. Jess felt a sense of relief at how easy it was to tell her about it. He didn't have to steel himself first, as he had to do even when he talked to McAllister about it.

"You see," he told her, "I had a Comanche wife."

"That's different," she said bitterly. "For some reason nobody thinks its wrong for a man off alone somewhere to get himself an Indian girl for a short while. Just so long as he leaves her behind when he goes on his way. Is that what you did?"

"She was my wife, Mrs. Graff. Her name was Singing Sky. She was like that—like her name. Somebody murdered her."

She looked at him differently then. Jess could see by the star shine that the sullen anger was gone from her face, as though she suddenly sensed the bond between them.

"Who killed her?"

"I don't know. I been looking for him for a year, ever since it happened. I think I know where he is, now. I'm gonna get him soon."

"Mr. Remsberg," Ellen said quietly, "you haven't found a new life for yourself either, have you?"

Jess started to build another cigarette. Suddenly he dropped the makings and rubbed his palms together hard. His hands were trembling.

"No," he told her. "I haven't."

In the darkness, each sensed the bond between them growing stronger.

Jess stared ahead, remembering vividly how he had found Singing Sky's body. After he'd been silent a long time, Ellen began to talk softly, to tell him her story as she'd been able to tell no one before: of her captivity among Chata's Chiricahua Apaches; of her red-haired son, a baby less than one year old now.

"I tried to escape from them. They always caught me. The last time I tried was less than a week before that cavalry company discovered Chata's camp. I took my son one night and slipped away. Chata sent out several bands after me. One of them led by my . . . by Chata's son, Nachee. I didn't have a chance. I didn't even have a horse."

"You wouldn't have had much chance of outdistancing them even if you did have a horse," Jess said. "Those Chiricahuas know how to trail. So Nachee found you and took you back?"

"No. The band that caught me wasn't the one Nachee was with. But they took me back to Chata's camp with them. Nachee wasn't there. All the warriors were out with Chata on a raid. The one that brought me back left me there and went off to join the raid. The next day that cavalry company hit Chata's camp."

"I heard. That's when you got that cut on your head."

"The Apaches are supposed to be cruel. But white men are no different. Those troopers . . . Nothing can justify what they did that morning. There weren't any warriors in the camp. They were all out with Chata. But that didn't mean anything to our brave army! The way they rampaged through that defenseless camp . . . killing old men, children, women, shooting and cutting down everyone in sight. You could see they were enjoying themselves."

"I don't think they enjoyed it, Mrs. Graff. Maybe some of them. Most just had their blood worked up for a fight, not knowing there weren't any warriors in Chata's camp. Most of 'em would be sick with themselves and what they did after it was over and they calmed down. I've seen it happen that way."

"They *did* enjoy it! Killing Indians that can't fight back—that's work for a real man, isn't it?" She touched the scar on her forehead. "The trooper that gave me this tried to cave in my skull with his rifle butt before he saw I was white. I was unconscious when the troopers took me away and brought me back. I didn't have a chance to take my son with me."

Her voice choked up. Jess knew she was fighting sobs as she relived what had happened, thought of her son.

"Mrs. Graff, if I was your husband, I'd take you far away from here, where you could start over again."

"There's nothing for me, anywhere. People look at me as if I'm dirty, evil. Everyone thinks any decent white woman would have preferred death to life as an Apache squaw. Maybe they're right."

"Death comes soon enough, seems to me. Especially out here. Anybody hurries it for any reason is a damn fool."

"People in this town don't feel that way about it."

"You and your husband could move someplace where people don't know about what happened."

"My husband would know," she said bitterly. "No matter where we went, he'd remember."

Jess thought of the way Millard Graff had received his wife back, and he could say nothing to that.

"So you see, Mr. Remsberg," Ellen said, "there's only one thing left to me. My son."

"You got to forget about the boy, Mrs. Graff. Apaches love kids. They'll treat him good."

"He's my son!"

"You're young. You'll have more children."

"No I won't. My husband hates . . ." She stopped herself and finished lamely: "There'll be no more children. I've to get to my son."

"You can't do that, Mrs. Graff. You've got to put that out of your head."

"I'm going to." Her voice was soft, but defiant. "I'm going to keep trying till I do it."

"If I was your husband, I'd see to it you didn't get away again."

"You're not my husband, though." She stood up suddenly. "I want to go home now. I'm tired."

Jess nodded and got to his feet. He lifted her up onto Lobo and swung himself into the saddle. He turned the dun back toward town.

After leaving Ellen Graff off at her house, Jess rode to the post. Stabling Lobo, he went to McAllister's room. The big lieutenant wasn't in. Jess bedded down in the extra bunk, lay there with his hands behind his head, staring up at the wooden rafters.

Ordinarily, he had the ability to put himself into a sleep instantly on lying down. But that night he didn't fall asleep for a long time. Once, stretching his arm down along his side, his hand touched the leather pouch that Gil McAllister had given him. His fingers stroked it slowly, as though what was in it were still part of someone alive. His mind and emotions were full of Singing Sky—and Ellen Graff. Somehow, the two of them were becoming twisted together in his mind.

FIVE

Dawn was a red blob pushing up over the distant hills. Its rust-gold glow, bringing a gentle warm breeze with it, struck long black shadows across the width of the parade ground, where Sergeant Ferguson was barking his troopers into formation with their mounts. Jess Remsberg came down off the Officers Row boardwalk carrying his carbine, bedroll and saddlebags. The saddlebags were heavy, were crammed with extra ammunition for his carbine and the long barreled .45 Colt, which was holstered against his right thigh. Helping to bulge those saddlebags were a pair of binoculars, a tin plate and cup, and lean emergency rations for when he was off on his own: hardtack, sugar, bacon, and coffee. Two canteens, filled to their brims, hung from his left shoulder. He wore new buckskin shirt and pants, bought with money Gil McAllister had advanced him from his scouting pay.

Jess paused for a moment to feel the air of expectancy coming to him from the assembling cavalrymen. It was their eagerness to be going somewhere—anywhere—that was stronger than nervousness about where they were going, and why. Jess had the same itch inside him, only with him it was stronger. Fort Duell was a goal that had special meaning for him.

He walked along the company barracks toward Lobo, already saddled and waiting for him at the hitchrack outside the quartermaster corrals. His limp was more pronounced

than usual that morning. He had drunk too much the night
before, and had slept too rigidly, not shifting position, with
his weight on his injured hip.

Lobo turned his sleek neck to nuzzle Jess as he tied on the
saddlebags and bedroll, and thrust the carbine into its boot.
As he hung the two canteens from the pommel, one on
either side, Jess saw Gil McAllister come out onto the deep-
shadowed headquarters veranda with Major Novak. Gil
stood there exchanging a last few words with the major,
while glancing out over the parade ground to see if
Ferguson had everything ready to ride.

Sergeant Ferguson shouted an order. His twenty-four
troopers settled stiffly into position. The lined-up horses
stamped impatiently, each held firm by the trooper at its
bridle bit. To one side waited the two big quartermaster
wagons, each with four mules in traces, each heavily loaded
with ammunition for Fort Duell. Behind them was the cook
wagon, its high hump of canvas covering cooking equip-
ment and enough food and barrels of water to last them
across five hundred miles of sun-scourged emptiness.

Jess tightened his saddle cinches and swung up onto Lobo
as a man in a black frock coat rode a strapping bay in
through the parade gate. It was Toller, the gambler. Toller
waved his arm to Jess and grinned.

"Told you I'd be going along!"

Jess raised a hand in mock salute and grinned back. There
was something about the gambler he liked. He'd forced
himself to forget the circumstances of their first brief
meeting.

A rattling rumble outside the gate caught Jess's attention.
Two stocky draft horses pulled a freight wagon in through
the gate. Millard Graff, working the reins, looked strong
and solid up on the driver's bench. Behind him, dark canvas
streched tight over the high load of goods he intended to sell
at Duell.

Jess watched thoughtfully as Graff maneuvered the
wagon to one side of the gate, pulled the horses to a halt, set
the brake, and climbed down to stretch his legs. Jess

hesitated a moment, then let his impulse rule him. Swinging down from his saddle, he limped over to Graff, who leaned against the side of his wagon lighting a cigar.

"Hello, Graff."

Graff looked up with a smile that vanished when he recognized Jess. He shook out his match and spoke flatly around the cigar clamped between his even teeth: "Hello. Ready to roll?"

Jess nodded, fighting the hesitation inside him again. Close up, Graff looked haggard this morning, with dark smudges under his eyes.

Jess said, "I heard you were going along with us."

Graff met Jess's eyes, searching for what Jess wanted of him. "That's right. I heard you were scout, since Tom Van's dead."

"You know," Jess told him, "you may not be able to get any kind of escort back this way for weeks, maybe months. You'll be stuck at Duell."

"I know."

Jess hesitated again, then said, "Maybe it ain't such a good idea, leaving your wife back here alone all that time. Considering everything."

Graff flinched, but his eyes continued to meet Jess's, though a slow flush grew under the tan of his handsome face.

"It don't matter now," Graff said evenly. "Ellen stole two horses and disappeared last night."

The shock of it was cold in the pit of Jess's stomach. "I didn't hear about that. Didn't you report it to post commander here?"

"Why should I?"

"Why?" Jess stared at Graff, amazed. "They'd've gone out after her. Now maybe she's got too much of a start. Why'n hell didn't you report it?"

Graff took the cigar out of his mouth and dropped it to the ground. His face was tight with shame and anger. "If it's any of your business, mister, there's no sense goin' after her if she wants to go. You brought her back once, didn't you?

So now she's gone again." Graff suddenly ground the cigar into the dust viciously with his heel. His face became twisted, ugly. "If she wants to go, she can go! Straight to hell for all I care!"

Jess went on staring at Graff, finding nothing to say, holding back the impulse to slam into the man. Graff must have read something in Jess's face, for suddenly his hand came up to rest on the butt of his holstered gun.

"*Is* it any of your business, mister?" Graff said. "Because if it is . . ."

Jess turned on his heel and walked slowly away from Graff, toward Lobo.

Ellen Graff was sure to be killed—either by the empty, dry distances or by the Apaches. The thought of it dug at him. The more he dwelled on it, the more deeply it disturbed him. He couldn't explain his feeling, but it was as though he were somehow responsible for her—as if part of him would die with her.

Glancing up at the headquarters veranda, Jess saw Gil shake hands with Major Novak, draw on his gloves, and stomp down the wooden steps to the parade ground. Jess started over to meet him, walking fast. He knew what he had to do now.

"Gil!"

Lieutenant McAllister halted and turned toward him. "All set, Jess. Let's go."

"Gil, I'm gonna ride on alone first, scout due south. I know your route. I'll swing back and pick you up along the way in a few days."

McAllister looked at him. "How come?"

"Maybe I can locate Chata's band for you. Check on how strong he is now. See if he's ready to come north yet. I'll want an extra horse to make good time."

McAllister narrowed his eyes thoughtfully, moved his huge shoulders restlessly under his blue service blouse. "Jess, are you thinking about going on to Duell without me? Getting to the man that had Singing Sky's scalp when I'm not along?"

Jess shook his head. "No. You got my word on that. I'll swing back in a few days and meet you along the route. Won't do any harm for me to see what's up ahead of you."

"All right. Get yourself another horse out of the corral. And if you get anywhere near Chata, be careful. What the hell, I don't have to tell you."

"That's right. You don't."

"Good luck." McAllister turned to Sergeant Ferguson and said, "Prepare to mount."

Jess headed for the corrals as Ferguson's yell rang out to the troopers: "Prepare to mount!"

Jess rode most of the morning before he gave up the hope of finding Ellen Graff's trail. The land that stretched away from him to the horizon was too open; there were no obvious paths. She could have made up her route as she went along.

After that he struck straight south for Sonora and Tres Castillos. Whatever route Ellen Graff chose, she was headed for Chata's hide-out. By doing the same, Jess could hope that their paths would finally converge on the other side of the border. She had a good start on him, which meant that she should reach Chata before he caught up with her. But Jess counted on the time she would have to spend in the Tres Castillos searching for Chata. . . .

Shortly after dawn of the second day, Jess came across sign of two shod horses headed south. Squatting on his heels, Jess studied the tracks. One horse was carrying a rider, the other was not. It could be Ellen.

He lost the tracks two hours later, where the horses had gone across a vast stretch of cracked earth baked too hard to take the print of a horse's hoof. Jess kept on toward Tres Castillos. He rode fast, alternating on Lobo and his spare horse to make better time without wearing either horse out. He had to catch up with Ellen before she got too deep into the Tres Castillos. If she got close enough to the Chiricahua camp, she wouldn't have to find Chata. Chata would find her.

* * *

Ellen sat on the hard ground atop a small hill blossoming with purple sand verbena and golden desert dandelions. Her hands trembled holding the canvas-wrapped canteen between them. On the slope of the hill below her, the two horses fed greedily on the flowers and high stands of tough grass. That was something, at least; they'd get moisture that way.

She had spotted this colorful hill earlier that day and headed straight for it, hoping to find a spring here. There was no spring. Anyway, not above ground; and she couldn't take the time to dig for one. Uncapping the canteen, she raised it to her lips and drank sparingly. Capping it again, she shook the canteen and listened to the water inside. After three days of riding, there wasn't much left.

She placed the canteen on her thighs and let her hands rest there with it, wishing they'd stop trembling. Raising her dirt-streaked, dust-caked face, Ellen stared at the high, blunted hills rising to the south. Over them rose the pointed peak of a higher red-rock mountain. Above the peak a massive, fat white cloud hung low in the light-blue sky. From the distance, it looked as if the cloud balanced on the point of that high peak.

Somewhere in that tangle of hills and canyons Chata's band waited.

The last time she had tried this, she'd become afraid and turned back long before getting this far. This time she was determined not to turn back.

Ellen stood up abruptly and went down to the horses. Mounting the saddled one, she started toward the hills, leading the other horse by a short rope. She found herself suddenly thinking of Jess Remsberg. He had said that the Apaches would kill her. Ellen persuaded herself that he was wrong. He didn't know Nachee.

Nachee was not the kind of man to love any woman, but he had liked her well enough that he wouldn't let his father kill her. Ellen knew she wouldn't escape from them again. They'd watch her too closely. But she would have her son with her once more. That was all she cared about. That, she told herself each time the doubts rose in her, was all that was left for her to care about.

There was only a couple of hours to go till dusk when Ellen, following a tortuous trail through the towering rock hills, suddenly found herself at the top of a slope that fell away into a tremendous canyon walled around by red and brown cliffs. Drawing in her mount, she scanned the canyon nervously. There was no sign of life, no movement. Halfway down the slope, a single massive tower of centuries-whitened rock rose hundreds of feet into the air, its top flattened off at exactly the same height as the rim of the cliffs surrounding the canyon. Saguaro cactus grew on the slope, sparse where Ellen was, more dense toward the bottom.

Sunlight glistened back from a slim thread wandering through the length of the canyon at the bottom. A stream. Water for herself and the horses. It would, Ellen decided, be the best place to camp for the night.

Kicking gently at her mount, Ellen started him down the slope, tugging along the other horse. The horses went slowly, feeling their way down the sandy surface. Ellen reached the towering sentinel of rock and rode down past it. The sudden sound of horses' hoofs behind her made Ellen rein sharply and jerk her head around.

She had tried to steel herself to expect it, but fear clutched her in a cold vise. She had to grab hold of the pommel for support.

There were two Apaches. They rode slowly down from behind the tower of rock and halted, one on either side of her. They carried rifles and wore knee-high moccasins and dirty loincloths. Each wore his sleek black hair long, held back by a flannel rag wound around his head and across his forehead. Each had a streak of yellow paint across his cheekbones and the bridge of his nose. Between the parallel lines of the paint and the flannel bands, their eyes stared out at her as though through masks. She didn't know either of them.

Reaching up quickly, Ellen pulled off her dirty, wide-brimmed hat, revealing her red hair to them.

"I am Flame," she told them in Chiricahua Apache, the words coming out halting and shaky. "I am Nachee's wife, come back. Take me to Chata."

The two Apache warriors glanced at each other, then back to her. One of them kicked his horse over against hers, pinning her leg between them. He reached out a dark bare arm and fingered a loose strand of Ellen's red hair. He grinned at her insolently and ran his fingers down her cheek, over her body.

"Nachee chose well," he said softly.

Ellen stiffened, and forced strength into her voice. "You will be punished for that. Take me to Chata."

The other Indian spoke suddenly. "Chata has spoken of her. Chata would wish to see her . . . before anything was done to her."

The first warrior nodded slowly. His hand went to Ellen's thigh, his fingers digging in cruelly. "Afterwards, this one will be mine."

"I belong to Nachee!" Ellen snapped. "If you touch me again, I will tell Nachee. He will kill you."

The Apache warrior slapped her suddenly across the face, hard. His hand caught her arm to keep her from falling from her saddle.

"Nachee is dead," he told her.

Ellen stared at him, more stunned by what he had said than by the blow that had left its imprint against the side of her face.

The other one seized her reins. "We will take her to Chata. What is done with her will be Chata's will."

Dazed, Ellen rode with them to the bottom of the canyon. There they turned to follow the stream. Ellen sat in her saddle listlessly. Her terror was gone. In its place was numbed resignation. She had counted on Nachee's desire for her to protect her. But Nachee was dead. How had he died? Chata had fled here to Mexico after the army trapped his warriors and wiped them out. Had Nachee been killed then?

However he had died, he was dead. Now her fate was in the hands of the wrathful Chata. . . .

It was almost dusk when the warriors took Ellen away from the stream and entered a maze of short, narrow canyons. For perhaps a mile, the steep cliffs walling their route were so close together that Ellen could have touched both sides at the same time by stretching out her arms. They went single file, one warrior ahead of Ellen and the other bringing up the rear, through obscuring darkness. Then the walls began to draw further apart again. Ellen's nostrils twitched as a familiar smell reached her—roasting antelope steaks and tule bulbs. An instant later they turned a corner and were in the camp.

Ellen was dragged down from her horse, pushed toward the center of the camp. She recognized some of the women, old men and children that crowded around to look at her. But not any of the young warriors. Their eyes were curious, filled with excitement and greedy viciousness. They left the fires to join the growing, noisy procession to their chief's wickiup.

Chata, drawn by the shouts of the women, came outside and stood waiting beside the pole-and-rope ramada enclosing his five ponies. He was a short, squat man, his former stockiness gone slack with age. He wore a patched shirt that fell halfway down his thick thighs. A belt of carbine cartridges was slung around his thick middle. His dirty gray hair hung long and straight to his shoulders, framing a wide face that resembled wrinkled mahogany. The eyes that dominated that face were unusually large, seeming to swallow whatever he looked at.

The two warriors brought Ellen before him, each holding one of her arms. A short, chopping motion of Chata's gnarled hands made them let go of her. For a long time the Chiricahua chief and the red-haired woman gazed at each other silently.

Chata was an old, bitter man, wracked with arthritis and filled with hate. There had been a time, long ago, when the Apache chiefs had accepted the Americans as allies against their natural enemies the Mexicans. But after the Mexicans were whipped and driven south into Mexico, the Americans turned out to be just as bad. They lied to the Apaches, tried to make them settle down on the San Carlos reservation, where malaria killed Indians by the scores. Chata had broken free and had fought the Americans ever since. For years he had roamed at will, raiding solitary ranches and farms, slaughtering small bands of travelers, giving the pursuing U.S. Army the slip each time.

But finally they had caught and trapped him in a blind canyon, wiping out most of his band. Chata himself had escaped, and had come here to the Tres Castillos, where the Mexican border protected him from the U.S. Army. He had sent out word for other Apaches with blood in their veins to join him.

Now his force was built up to forty-five warriors. He was ready to head north of the border again to take up his raiding in Arizona, New Mexico and Texas. Other Apaches would join him as his raids were successful, and he would drive the white man from this land, his land. He was an old man, cunning and cruel, possessed by his vision of vengeance and triumph.

The silent waiting unnerved Ellen. At last she spoke, nervously. "I have come back."

Before the impassive stare of Chata's large dark eyes, Ellen's answering stare broke. She lowered her eyes.

"Do you not look about you, Flame?" Chata's voice was low. "Do you not wish to gaze again upon Nachee, my son?"

Ellen did not raise her eyes to meet his. "I know he is dead. Your warriors spoke of it to me."

"He is dead," Chata agreed. "He died seeking you. His pony fell into a canyon and killed my son."

Ellen forced the words. "I am grieved that your son, my husband, is dead."

"Ah! You lie. It is your fault that my son is dead."

She looked up then, quickly, the fear growing colder

within her. "That is not true! I did not wish his death. You say that he fell . . ."

"He died following you. He died because you ran away. I will think now on a fitting punishment for that."

It was useless to argue with Chata. Ellen felt her body sag. "My son," she muttered weakly. "Is my son well?"

Chata gazed at her a moment longer. Then he jerked his head toward his wickiup.

Ellen took a hesitant step toward the blanket covering the wickiup entrance. Chata made no move to stop her. Ellen pulled aside the blanket and bent her head as she stepped inside.

The boy sat on the ground before the little cookfire with one of Chata's young wives. He was a little less than one year old, big for his age, with light red hair and blue eyes. Ellen fell to her knees beside him, murmuring softly, her eyes filling with tears. The boy looked up at her, frightened at first. Then, as Ellen reached out to stroke his round cheek, recognition dawned in his eyes. He smiled with delight and quickly held out his short arms to her.

Chata's young wife jumped up angrily and pushed Ellen away. "Do not touch him! He is *my* son now!"

Ellen sprang up like a cat, her fist lashing out and catching the Indian woman square in the face. The woman fell back screaming.

Chata stepped inside the wickiup. Ellen scooped up her baby and cradled him in her arms, her face tight with anger and fear. The baby began to cry.

Chata's glance took in what had happened instantly. A slice of his hand through the air cut off his wife's screams. "The boy is the son of Flame," he snapped at her. "It is right that she should care for him . . . while she still lives."

He jerked his hand toward the entrance. His young wife scrambled to her feet and hurried out. Chata looked at Ellen.

"My young warriors lust for you," he told her. "I have told them it cannot be. You belong to my dead son."

Ellen rocked her crying baby, soothing him, and said nothing.

"If I am killed in battle, my warriors will have their way with you. But they will not touch you while I live. You will live in my wickiup, be close to me as we move north. Nachee is buried in the Sangre de Cristo mountains. You will be allowed to live until we reach the place where my son is buried. Nachee was seeking for you when he found death. I will give you to him. I will bury you with him."

Ellen had felt too much terror. Now her senses were too blunted to feel more. She looked down at the baby in her arms, not at Chata, as she spoke. "You will kill me?"

"No," Chata said. "I will not kill you. You will be alive when I bury you in the grave of my son."

SIX

Jess Remsberg lay belly-down under a tangle of ocotillo bushes on the edge of the cliff, studying Chata's camp in the canyon below through his binoculars. Chata's band was moving out—warriors, women, children; everyone. Jess had reached this hidden vantage point during the night. Since the sun had come up less than an hour before, he had been watching the preparations for abandoning this camp.

It was a good thing he had decided to ride this far south. He had learned something that the army should know. He had counted the number of Chata's warriors. Chata was now stronger than he had ever been and his breaking this camp meant only one thing: he was moving north to begin his bloody raids again.

The fact that he was taking women and children with him—moving everything—meant that Chata intended to establish another camp far north across the border, probably in that favorite Apache hiding place, the almost impenetrable canyons between the Little Colorado and the Mongollons. From there his warriors would raid the entire Southwest, striking swiftly across hundreds of miles, vanishing at the approach of General Crook's large pursuing force.

But Jess still did not know what concerned him more. Through his binoculars, he studied the women now as they hauled family belongings out of the wickiups for the journey north. One after another he looked at them through the next hour, hope growing in him as he failed to spot the one he was looking for. At last everyone was assembled, ready to travel, and still he had not spotted her.

Then a new figure emerged from the largest wickiup. A woman. Jess focused the field glass on her, and felt himself go limp. It was Ellen Graff. Even at this distance, there was no mistaking that red hair of hers. She carried a baby in a wide band of cloth slung over her shoulders. The baby's hair was red, too.

He was too late. He had lost his race with Ellen. Until now, he hadn't been sure. He had picked up Ellen's trail below the border and followed it into this maze of canyons. Then he had lost it again. His only hope had been that she was still wandering around here somewhere, unable to make contact with Chata. Now there was no hope; Chata had her.

Jess didn't waste time thinking over schemes to get her away from Chata. There were about forty-five warriors with Chata, and Jess was one lone man.

Jess crawled backward through the ocotillo bushes till he was out of sight of anyone looking up from the canyon. He lay on his stomach for a few minutes, turning his head carefully to study the rock humps around him, the high ridge behind him. His ears strained for any sound. His heart was thudding heavily against the ground. Any man that got this close to a band of Apache warriors without being afraid was a fool.

At last he rose to his knees, hunched over, and slipped the Colt from his holster. With the Colt in one hand and the carbine in the other, he made his way on his knees to a break in the ridge twenty yards away, along a route where he was screened by boulders and bushes. Inside the break in the ridge, he paused, holding his breath and listening. Then he stood up and stepped through quickly, Colt up and ready. There was no one in sight.

Jess set off, hiking fast toward the spot where he'd left Lobo and the army horse half a mile back. His wide gray eyes scanned the ridges around him ceaselessly. Every few moments he turned his head as he hurried along, and glanced back the way he'd come.

He was almost up to the twin boulders behind which he'd left his mounts when he saw the two mounted Chiricahua warriors come around the corner of a shale slide a quarter of a mile to his left.

Jess broke into a sprint, favoring his limp automatically, out of habit. He scrambled up over the boulders. A rifle spanged. Chips flew off the boulder inches from Jess's hand. The two Indians split the air with their wild blood-cries as their ponies pounded after him.

An instant later, Jess was down behind the protective boulders, swinging up onto the saddled Lobo, seizing the army horse's lead rope. He kicked Lobo hard, got around a jut in a canyon wall, and went racing for the protection of the blunted hills to the north.

By the time the two warriors were in sight again behind him, Jess had almost a mile lead on them and was pushing ahead full speed out into the open. They came after him now in silent pursuit, not firing again. The distance was too great for accuracy from horseback, and the Apaches didn't have any bullets to waste. They concentrated on running him down, narrowing the distance.

For almost three miles Jess pushed Lobo to the limit without losing ground or gaining it between him and his pursuers. Then, without stopping, he hauled up the army horse alongside and managed the switchover. He rode the army horse bareback, clinging to its mane, giving Lobo a rest from carrying his weight. Jess covered another few miles before switching back to Lobo.

The two Apache warriors had no extra horses with them. After an hour, their mounts began to falter with exhaustion, falling back. Another hour and they were lost to sight, far behind Jess.

For the rest of the day, Jess worked his way north through the hills. He was on the other side of them by nightfall. He camped in a bone-dry stream bed. There was no wood in sight for a fire, so Jess dug a small hole with his knife, clubbed some dry bunchgrass together in it, and set it aflame. It wasn't much of a fire, but it was enough to warm the coffee in his tin cup. He ate three hard biscuits soaked in the coffee, and two strips of raw bacon. Then he spread his ground sheet, rolled up in his blanket, and fell instantly asleep.

He was up two hours before dawn. A spare breakfast, and he was on his way again.

Ellen Graff stayed with him all the way. He hadn't given up the thought of getting her away from Chata. There might be a chance—only one—in the near future. But he couldn't do it alone. He would be with the army whenever it tangled with Chata. And he would have just one purpose: to get past Chata's warriors in the confusion and grab Ellen away from them. It was a slim hope, but he clung to it.

His preoccupation with Ellen Graff disturbed him. It wasn't that he had forgotten about the man in Duell who'd had Singing Sky's hair. His purpose was still there: he was going to get the man who killed Singing Sky; that man was going to die. But now that purpose had been pushed to the back of his mind.

Jess came across the tracks of McAllister's troopers and wagon train two hundred miles from Fort Duell. He stopped for a moment to count back in his mind. It was eight days since he had left Fort Creel. McAllister was making better time than he'd expected. Jess followed the tracks.

It was shortly after dusk when he sighted McAllister's campfires atop a hill ahead of him. Jess thought it over and decided he might as well spend the night alone. There was nothing to be gained by getting to McAllister that night. Not enough to take a chance on a frightened sentry's firing at him in the darkness.

Jess rode in at dawn, in time for breakfast. McAllister strode over with his cup of coffee in one big hand as Jess dismounted.

"Jess! I thought you forgot about coming back."

The relief plain on McAllister's face told Jess that the big lieutenant had imagined he had been killed.

"I was down having a look at Chata," Jess told him. He limped over to the cook wagon. "How about some breakfast?"

"Chata?" Sergeant Ferguson, already mounted, reined over his horse to stare down at Jess. Others crowded up to the cookwagon too, Graff and Toller among them.

Toller grinned at him and remarked, "You don't look as though you've left any part of you behind. Congratulations."

Jess nodded and took a gulp of scalding coffee. "My luck was better than my good sense, I guess."

McAllister laid a heavy hand on Jess's shoulder. "You mean you saw sign of him? Or Chata himself?"

"I saw him. Not close enough to spit at, but close enough. And I saw what he had with him." Jess looked at McAllister over the rim of his cup. He lowered the cup and said seriously, "Gil, he's got about forty-five armed bucks with him, by my count. Maybe more I didn't see."

McAllister whistled thoughtfully. "If he's that strong, he'll be ready to come north again any day now."

"Already has," Jess told him. "He started out almost four days ago."

"On a raid?"

"No. Took his whole camp with him." Jess glanced at Millard Graff, then back to McAllister. He gulped more of the coffee. "Women and kids, everybody and everything."

"Where was he headed?"

"I didn't stick around long enough to know. Not for sure."

"The Mongollons?" McAllister suggested.

Jess nodded. "That'd be the guess I'd stick with till something proved different. With the families along, he's got to set up another permanent camp before he does anything else, the way I see it."

Abruptly, McAllister started for his horse, motioning for Jess to follow. Toller and Graff, being the only men not

under orders, trailed along. McAllister drew a map from his
saddlebags, opened it against his saddle. He glanced at the
two civilians, a flicker of annoyance showing in his face.
But he didn't shoo them away.

"Show me where Chata's camp was," he said to Jess.

Jess marked a tiny X on the map with his thumbnail.
McAllister ran a thick finger from the X to the center of the
area between the Little Colorado and the Mongollons.
"Any reason why Chata wouldn't head straight there, the
shortest route?"

"No reason. You can't be sure, though."

"I know. But if Chata is taking the shortest way, that'd
put him about a hundred miles from us right this minute.
Maybe less."

Jess rubbed a wet palm slowly against the holster of his
Colt. "Gil," he said quietly, "Chata has almost fifty
fighting men with him. You've got twenty-five. Twenty-
eight, counting Graff, Toller and me."

"Wait a minute!" Millard Graff blurted. "Lieutenant,
you're not aiming to tangle with Chata with me along, are
you?"

McAllister gave the freighter a flat stare. "I wasn't
talking to you, Graff. If you're going to eavesdrop, at least
keep your goddamn mouth shut."

Jess knew that when McAllister got that sound to his
voice, the man he was aiming it at better pull in his ears.
But Graff didn't know McAllister.

"Listen," Graff persisted, "you're talking about my life.
I didn't come along to get run into any fight with Apaches.
You're supposed to be headed for Fort Duell."

McAllister's face flamed a deeper red. For a moment,
Jess thought he was going to hit Graff. But the officer got
hold of himself.

"I didn't invite you along, Graff. You wanted to come.
Now if you're anxious to get to Duell before the rest of us,
you just climb up on that wagon of yours and get going."

"Alone? Do you think I'm crazy?"

"Don't ask me. That's your problem." McAllister turned

on the gambler. "Well, Toller? You busting with things to say, too?"

Toller shrugged unhappily. "I didn't figure on fighting any Indians unless I had to. But you're the boss. As you've pointed out, you didn't invite me to join you."

"All right, then. Now Mr. Remsberg and me are going to have a private talk. Private. That means keep the hell away from us."

McAllister turned on his heel and walked past the grazing, roped-in horses toward a big flat rock on the side of a short hill. Jess followed and sat down on the rock beside him. He rested his wrists on his knees, staring off at the horizon to the south, waiting.

"Jess," McAllister said, "I've made up my mind. I'm going to strike south, hit Chata by surprise."

Jess plucked a long blade of grass and braided it through his thin fingers. "Chata don't surprise so easy, Gil. And twenty-five to forty-five—that's bad odds."

"You've got to figure on the fact that Chata has women and children with him, Jess. That'll slow him up plenty. He can't hit and run so fast. Whatever he does, he'll be hampered by those women and kids, and by all the baggage. And we should be able to pick our time and place to hit him. We know he's out here. He doesn't know we are."

"You've got some points there," Jess admitted. He looked at McAllister's tense face and forced a grin. "You sure do like the idea of getting your glory in one big hunk, don't you?"

McAllister blushed, then laughed. "Maybe. But what I'm thinking makes good military sense, too."

"Yeah. And it's sure to get you a quick promotion. If it works. And if you live through it."

McAllister shrugged. "Well, we can only die once, Jess. Might as well go trying to do what's right."

"Sure. Only there's a man I've got to see in Duell before I die. Have you really thought this out, Gil? You're taking a chance on losing all your troopers—and losing those ammunition wagons to Chata."

"You think I'm dumb enough to let that happen?"

"I think you'd be playing it smarter if you just kept on for Duell. Then you could come back with a force big enough to tackle Chata."

"By the time we'd get to Duell—and by the time Colonel Foster rode out again with a full cavalry company—Chata'd be safe up north in those canyons. We'd maybe never find his camp in that country. And if we did, you can bet Chata would have it somewhere where we'd bleed plenty trying to get at it."

Jess shook his head. "You've got it all figured out. I've got to admit I wasn't thinking that far ahead. But do you really think you've got enough men to lick forty-five Apache warriors with Chata doing their thinking for them?"

"I don't know whether I can lick Chata with the men I've got, but at least I can catch him and pin him down out here for a few days. I'm going to send Corporal Harrington on to Duell on the fastest horses we've got. If I can just hold Chata still until Colonel Foster shows up with a full company, there won't be any more Chata to worry about."

Jess grinned. "Gil, you'll be a general sure enough before you're through."

He stood up with McAllister. He could have argued more, but he knew he didn't really want to stop McAllister from doing this. The thought of Ellen Graff was too strong in him. The sooner they hit Chata, the more chance there was of her still being alive.

McAllister yelled: "Harrington!"

The corporal came up on the double, snapped McAllister a smart salute.

"Corporal," McAllister said, "I'm going to assign you two good horses. I want you to carry a dispatch for Colonel Foster to Fort Duell. And I don't want you to stop on the way. Not to sleep, not to eat, not to anything. You understand?"

"You bet. Sir."

Jess looked over Corporal Harrington. He was a short, thin man in his early thirties, tough of face and hard of body. He had a drawl that sounded like Cap Rock, Texas. Jess had a hunch that those two horses were going to have the hell ridden out of them before they reached Duell.

"Very good," McAllister said. "Come with me."

As McAllister and Corporal Harrington started away together, Jess looked around till he spotted Millard Graff over by his freight wagon. Jess walked slowly over to him.

"Graff."

The blond freighter turned, his face sullen. "Yeah?"

"I saw your wife."

Nerves around Graff's eyes jumped. His face went slack. "You . . . was she . . ." He left it unfinished.

"She was alive, five days ago. She was in Chata's camp. Had her son with her."

Graff turned his back on Jess and pretended to busy himself with tightening one of the freight ropes. "So she made it," he said bitterly.

Jess told him: "There's a chance we could get to her, if we're gonna hit Chata's band. Want to talk it over?"

"She's where she wanted to be," Graff said softly, not turning back to Jess. "Do her a favor, and me a favor. Let her be."

SEVEN

Lieutenant Gilbert McAllister quartered the ridge and drew his tall buckskin to a halt on the narrow, rock-rubble crest. He hadn't pushed the buckskin hard up the steep incline, but the horse was sweat-slick and breathing fast from the scorching sun directly overhead, its flames pulsing in the heavy, motionless air. McAllister's uniform was soaked. The seat of his pants stuck wetly to his saddle. His eyes stung with the salt of perspiration trailing down his forehead from the hatband that seemed overtight, as though his head were swollen with the heat. He licked wet salt from his cracked lips and gazed westward across ten miles of sage-brush flat towards a long network of high, on-running ridges.

The flat shimmered with dust and heat haze. No live thing moved anywhere on it. Impatience gnawed at McAllister. Jess should have been back before this with a report on Chata's movements. He'd been gone two days now.

McAllister glanced back down the long incline falling away from the ridge to the wide pass below. Through that pass moved the blue column of his troopers, riding south, followed by the wagons. The sounds of their passing reached up thinly to the big lieutenant: the jingling of ring-bits and breaststrap buckles, the rattle of wagon wheels, the clop of horses' hoofs against the hard ground. Far off from both sides and both ends of the column moved the single outriders, keeping just within sight, as McAllister had instructed.

They'd been moving this way for three days, zigzagging slowly south over an area which should have brought them by now across Chata's route. McAllister began to fear that Jess's prediction was correct.

Jess had ridden out and back on the first day. He had returned with disturbing news. He'd come across signs of a single Indian pony. As near as Jess could make out, the pony had been ridden up from the south, had stopped within sight of McAllister's oncoming column, and then doubled back south.

In Jess's opinion, that meant an Apache was out scouting far in advance of Chata's band. The scout would race back to Chata with the news that a cavalry column was arrowing down to intercept him. Chata could then do one of two things: pick a strong spot from which to ambush McAllister as he rode south; or make a wide detour around McAllister's line of march and avoid contact.

The fact that Chata had women, children and baggage with him argued for his avoiding a fight at this time, by taking a long swing around McAllister. On the other hand, the Apache scout would have informed Chata that he outnumbered this cavalry company almost two to one.

"And one other thing," Jess had pointed out. "That Apache's gonna tell Chata about our wagons."

"There's no way," McAllister had said, "that Apache could know we've got ammunition in two of them."

"Sure. But we've got four loaded wagons. Whatever's in them, it has to be some kind of supplies for fighting men. Chata can figure that out. And he's got fighting men of his own he has to supply."

"So you figure Chata will try to ambush us."

"I don't know. I'm not smart enough to do Chata's thinking for him. But there's one thing I'd sure be willing to predict."

"What's that?"

"We're not gonna come on him by surprise, as you planned. We'll be lucky if it ain't the other way round."

"That's your job, Jess. Go see what he's up to."

"See you!" Jess had raised a hand in salute, and headed south on Lobo to follow the tracks of that Apache scout, figuring on their leading him to Chata.

That was two days ago. Jess should have returned by now.

McAllister gazed westward at the line of distant ridges. If Chata were still coming straight on north, they'd have run into him by now. McAllister's guess was that Chata was trying to avoid the cavalry as long as he had families and baggage with him, and would fight only if he had to. If that were so, Chata would probably be swinging west in his northward move. That way he could keep out of sight, keep those ridges between him and McAllister.

McAllister had to admit that he was less sure what he was doing was right than he had been three days back. Perhaps the best thing now would be to turn back. Corporal Harrington would have reached Fort Duell by now with his dispatch. If he turned back now, he'd meet Colonel Foster somewhere between here and Duell. Then they would go after Chata with the numerical odds in favor of the army.

There'd be no discredit in doing that. No credit, either. No promotion. McAllister wanted a promotion.

He thought of silken-haired Sarah Nimier, waiting at Duell for his return. A promotion would be a nice wedding present for her. Not that Sarah was the kind of girl who expected or demanded that her husband be a big man. Being just the man he was, that was enough for Sarah. She's made it plain. There were plenty of men with more rank and money who'd courted Sarah. Even Colonel Foster himself, being a widower, had showed interest till it became obvious she'd decided on the man she wanted.

Strangely, the very fact that Sarah didn't demand anything of him made McAllister all the more eager to do better by her than she'd expected he could. The more rank and pay you had, the better life was out here for your wife and kids.

McAllister took off his campaign hat and wiped his sleeve across his burning forehead. He settled the hat again, adjusted the chin strap, and stared again at the distant network of ridges, forcing Sarah out of his mind. Those ridges seemed to invite him. The longer he looked at them, the more convinced he became that Chata's band was moving north on the other side of them.

If he headed back now and joined up with Colonel Foster, Chata might get too much of a lead on them. And if they did catch Chata, it would be with Colonel Foster in command. Foster would get all the credit. But if McAllister beat Chata alone, or even just held him here till Colonel Foster showed up . . .

McAllister swung the reins and started his buckskin back down the incline to his moving column.

"Sergeant Ferguson!"

The plump, innocent-eyed sergeant swung his mount over to meet him.

"Yes, sir?"

"There's a break through this ridge about half a mile ahead of us. We'll cut through it and swing west."

"Yes, sir."

"There's a chain of hills ten miles west. I'm convinced the Chiricahuas are on the other side of those hills."

"Yes, sir." Ferguson hesitated. "Sir?"

"Yes?"

"Jess Remsberg is due back any time now, ain't he? Shouldn't we maybe . . ."

"That's just it. He was due back by now. He isn't back. Let's go, Sergeant!"

The line of mounted cavalrymen and the four wagons turned west through the break and rode out across the sagebrush flat. Acid dust kicked up by horses' hoofs rose to choke McAllister's nostrils and bite at his eyes. He raised his kerchief to cover his nose and mouth, narrowed his eyes as much as he could and still see. He heard his men begin to cough, spit and curse.

The column was halfway across the flat when McAllister saw his south outrider racing in.

"Sergeant Ferguson!"

But Ferguson had already seen, was detaching himself from the column. Ferguson rode south a hundred yards, halted, and slipped his carbine out of its boot. He raised the rifle high, swinging it back and forth. The outrider drew in his horse and raised his own carbine, pointing it straight up.

One rider, approaching from the south. McAllister drew up his buckskin beside Sergeant Ferguson.

"Must be Remsberg," Ferguson suggested. The outrider was swinging back to his station.

McAllister nodded. "Hope so. Take the column, Sergeant." He kicked his buckskin to action and trotted him toward the distant outrider.

A horse and rider appeared, paused for a moment beside the outrider, and rode on toward the column. McAllister identified the black-maned coyote dun before he could make out Jess. They met half a mile from the column.

Jess looked weary to the core. He sat his saddle lumpishly, shoulders slumping as though too heavy for his lean torso to support. Over the bones of his face the skin was drawn tight. His gray eyes were enflamed by sun and dust.

"Hi, Gil. Been out of water since sun-up."

McAllister uncapped his canteen and passed it over. Jess drank from it sparingly. Swinging down stiff from the saddle, he poured some water into his palm and wet Lobo's nostrils and mouth, then let the horse lap up a few mouthfuls. McAllister waited edgily till Jess handed back the canteen and remounted.

"Find Chata's trail?"

Jess nodded, squinted from the moving column to the westward hills and buttes. "Seems like you don't need me to scout for you. You figured it out by yourself."

"They're on the other side of those hills?"

"They're *in* the hills. Camped."

"Waiting for me?"

"Guess so. Got everybody camped down in a dry gully. You couldn't squeeze more'n one trooper at a time through to that gully."

McAllister scanned the approaches between the flat humps and ridges. The hills were mostly solid, wind-corroded rock, with no vegetation on them. "Chata knows he's got to fight me. That's a smart place to do it in."

"Must be water in there somewhere," Jess said. "I never found any. Apaches know where every drop of water is in a million miles. Pass on the information generation after generation. Never tell anybody but another Apache."

"So Chata holes up his women and kids where I can't get at them in there. That leaves his warriors free to fight with nothing weighing 'em down."

"Yeah. You want to fight him now, you've got to do it on his terms. Place and conditions picked by him to be against you—on top of which he's got twice the fighting men you've got."

McAllister nodded and continued to stare thoughtfully at the vast tangle of upheaved rock.

After a moment, Jess told him softly: "Chata gets up into the Mongollons, he's gonna play hell with this whole country. He's up here for blood, Gil."

"That's what we're here for," McAllister said absently, his mind on something else. "To see he's stopped before he starts."

"You're already too late for sixteen immigrants."

McAllister looked at him. "What happened?"

"Little wagon train. I found 'em a day after Chata did. All dead. Women, kids, babies. Everyone. With the usual Chiricahua trimmings." Jess spat, but couldn't get rid of the taste in his mouth. He thought again of how much he hated this land. He longed to head east to some city where no one needed to carry a gun, and you worried only about dying of old age.

McAllister's face was taut as he stared at the hills. "Chata has to be stopped. Right here."

Jess shook his head. "Chata outnumbers you two to one. You go into those canyons after him, he'll wipe you out."

"I know that. I'm not going in there after him. Corporal Harrington must have reached Duell by now. Colonel Foster'll be on his way. When he gets here, we'll be strong enough to go in after Chata. All Chata has to do is stay in those hills a few more days, and we've got him."

"He's not that dumb, Gil."

"He doesn't know Foster is on his way with more troops."

"Maybe not. But he'll figure it out pretty quick if you just sit out here and wait."

McAllister nodded. "Okay. We keep watch. He can't move his whole camp out without your spotting it. If he just stays in there, I'll wait for Foster. If he moves north, I'll hit him as soon as he's out of those hills. I'll hit him when he's got his women and children with him."

"He'll still outnumber you."

"I'm going to hold him, Jess, not fight him on his terms. I'll strike straight at the women and children, cut them off from the warriors, shove 'em back into the hills with us. Chata won't run off without his families. And he won't be able to slam into us all-out for fear of killing his own people that're with us. Whatever he tries to do to pry us loose from his women and children, it'll take time. All I got to do is hold him off till Foster shows up."

Jess pursed his lips thoughtfully.

"Well," McAllister snapped, "how's it sound to you?"

"Good," Jess admitted. "Only I can't believe Chata'll let you do it."

"What can he do about it? If he stays in those hills till Foster gets here, we've got him. If he moves out, I hit his weak point—the families he's dragging along with him."

"He could come out of those hills with just his warriors, Gil. Slam into us, wipe us out. Then bring out his women and kids and head north before Foster shows up."

"Sure. But if he comes out of those hills to fight me, it's going to be on *my* terms. In a place I pick. Let's go."

McAllister raced his buckskin back toward the moving column. Jess set Lobo to a lope behind him.

McAllister was already snapping orders at Sergeant Ferguson when Jess got there. The column—the mounted troopers and the four wagons—picked up speed. The big lieutenant galloped up ahead to lead the way, sending back his forward outrider to join the column. Jess came up alongside McAllister, kept pace with him. Glancing over, Jess saw the deep, hard furrows alongside McAllister's thinned-out mouth, between his thick eyebrows.

The hard, dusty surface of the flat merged into soft sand as they approached the hills. They had to slow down as their horses sank ankle deep. The sand rolled away ahead of them in gently rising dunes, all the way to the looming rocks.

McAllister pointed. "Jess, that hill over there."

Jess nodded, looking at it. It was more of a butte, solid rock, its high top flattened out. The incline on one side of it was gradual enough for horses to be dragged up slowly. It rose to one side of a wide-mouthed canyon leading into the heart of the hills.

"Good place for a stand," Jess said. "You get on top, Chata'd play hell trying to get up at you. His bucks would have to come up slowly, with no cover. You'd pick them off easy."

"That's what I figure, Jess. Good place to outwait Chata."

"If he isn't already up there himself. Or on the other side of it, waiting."

"He could be, I know. Up to you, Jess, to find out. If he is on that hill, we'll make a dash for that canyon over to the left, there. Before he can catch us, we can be up in those rocks, barricaded. We'll have the protection of the rocks. He'll have to come at us out in the open."

"Like I said a few days back, Gil. You'll be a general yet."

McAllister didn't smile. He'd tried to think of everything Chata might have thought of. He hoped he had.

"Wait here," McAllister told Jess, and doubled back to

the column. He had Ferguson signal the outriders to come
in. They joined the column as it came up to where Jess
waited, nervously studying the ridges, rocks and canyon
entrances. His throat tightened with the oppressive empty
silence. There was only the level sands stretching away
from him, and the gigantic rock formations rising in blocks,
mounds and turrets against the sky. Nowhere was there a
sign of an Apache. Only the beckoning silence and
emptiness.

McAllister was beside him again. "All right, Jess. You
go on ahead and scout that hill. We'll come on after you. If
you see anything fire a shot, and we'll kick hell out of the
horses getting to cover."

Tension mounted in Jess as he drew out his carbine and
nudged Lobo across the soft sand toward the butte. This was
the part of being an army scout that scared him most: riding
a far point alone, serving as bait or a warning signal. Asking
to get shot full of holes so those coming up behind him
could scatter for cover when it happened. His eyes darted
from shadow to shadow among the overlooming rocks as he
neared them. His carbine was up, his finger against the
trigger guard. He was filled with an absolute certainty that
Chata's marksmen were up there in those rocks somewhere
ahead of him, watching him come on toward them,
narrowing the range for them. He could feel rifle sights
centering on his chest, his face.

When at last he reached the massive side of the butte, its
bulk hiding him from the rest of the rocks momentarily, he
drew a quick, ragged breath. He looked up, half expecting
to see a rifle snout poking down at him from the top.
Nothing happened.

Jess slid out of his saddle. Still carrying the carbine
cradled in his right arm, he took hold of the reins with his
left hand and started climbing the steep slope, tugging Lobo
along. In five minutes he was on the top. And there was no
one there.

It was mounded and crevassed up there, and strewn with
small stones and boulders. There was plenty of room for the

army column, horses, wagons and all. Dropping the reins, Jess scouted the edges, seeing that there were no Apaches waiting on any side of the butte. Satisfied about that, he scanned the other rock faces of the nearest hills, but saw nothing alarming. He shook his head, puzzled. This kind of luck was hard to believe in connection with a famed desert fighter like Chata. But there it was.

Jess walked back to the edge facing the flat, looked down at the approaching cavalry column, moving slowly toward him across the deep sands. He started to raise his arm, to wave them on to the butte.

At that moment the sand on both sides of the column erupted. Mounds of sand flew up and aside with the blankets they'd covered, revealing the heads, shoulders, arms and aimed rifles of thirty Apache warriors, fifteen on each side of the trapped column.

Thirty rifles crashed in a ragged, point-blank volley, their bullets smashing into the stunned cavalrymen.

And while screams, yells and the meshed reports of the first slaughtering barrage still hung in the air, fifteen mounted Chiricahua warriors came howling out of the mouth of the nearest canyon and thundered head on against McAllister's decimated command.

EIGHT

McAllister, his ears stuffed with the explosions of rifles on either side of him, saw a trooper's face gush blood, felt lead whip past his eyes, heard the screams of men and animals behind him. In the split second before he could gather himself to act, he knew how completely Chata had outwitted him. He'd expected an ambush, but not out here where no ambush seemed possible.

Chata had seen the dust of the column coming across the flat, while that dust had kept McAllister from seeing how Chata swiftly set about preparing for him. Chata had dug two-thirds of his warriors into the sand on either side of the column's approach. Each warrior had covered his head, shoulders and rifle with a blanket, over which the sand was then pushed. With only a tiny hole left open for the warrior to see and breathe through, he was totally invisible until he magically arose from the sands a few feet from the troopers. They had let Jess ride straight through them, and he hadn't seen a thing.

McAllister whirled his buckskin, automatically snapping up his service revolver and firing it into a yelling Apache face. The Apache fell backwards with his teeth smashed in by the bullet. The horse behind McAllister was down, kicking its death agony, its rider pinned dead under it. The buckskin stumbled against the fallen horse, almost throwing McAllister, then shied off.

The sand-holed Apaches on both sides of the column

were firing rapidly, independently, taking a terrible toll of troopers and army horses. The mounted warriors who'd charged out of the canyon at the first volley were almost on top of the squirming mass of men and horses.

"The wagons!" McAllister yelled, pointing to the boulder-strewn base of a hill to his right. "Get the wagons into the rocks!"

The buckskin coughed and collapsed suddenly. McAllister threw himself free of the saddle just in time to keep his leg from being pinned, landed with a spine-wrenching jolt against his shoulder, and came up onto his knees with his revolver blasting the nearest Apache. A second later he was on his feet, only to be knocked spinning by a glancing blow from the side of a stampeding horse.

Dazed momentarily, he lay flat on his back and caught the blurred image of a bare-torsoed warrior swinging a long-bladed knife at him. In the same instant, a rifle barrel arched through the air and caved in the back of the warrior's head. The Indian fell across McAllister's chest. McAllister heaved the body away and scrambled to his feet. Sergeant Ferguson was bending sideways in his saddle, reaching for his hand.

McAllister started to take Ferguson's hand, then saw a riderless army sorrel milling about a few feet away. He reached the sorrel in two leaps, caught its reins and saddlehorn, and vaulted up on its back. His revolver was gone. Swinging the sorrel around, he spotted a fallen carbine and pushed the horse toward it. Leaning down, he snatched up the carbine, levered a load into the chamber, and glanced around at his wrecked command.

Three of the wagons were already on their way to the boulders. The third, the cookwagon, was stationary, one of its mules down in the traces, dead.

"Cut that mule away!" he screamed, and headed straight for it.

At that moment, the fifteen mounted Apaches careened into his surviving troopers. McAllister knocked one Apache rider off his pony with a carbine bullet, saw one of his troopers collapse forward in his saddle and slide to the

ground. Drumming in on the heels of the mounted attack
force came a string of riderless ponies led by two young
Indian boys. The Apaches who had sprung the ambush from
their sand holes now turned and sprinted for those ponies,
leaping onto their backs. McAllister drew bleak pleasure
from the fact that there were at least ten less of them now
than there had been when they'd magically blossomed from
the sands.

Desperately, McAllister tried to re-form the remnants
of his troops to seize the initiative from Chata. But
the Chiricahuas didn't give him the breather necessary
to accomplish this. Chata's moves followed one another
with clockwork precision. The fifteen mounted warriors
slammed into the tangled, milling column, bounced away
from it at an angle, then wheeled back for another slam.
When they came the second time, they were reinforced by
the other newly mounted Apaches.

McAllister managed to bunch his surviving troopers as
they beat off the second mounted attack. He drew them
slowly back toward the rocks, fighting a rear-guard action to
give the wagons time to reach the protective boulders at the
base of the hill. Over at the cookwagon, Sergeant Ferguson
had finally cut away the dead mule. Ten mounted Apaches
had detached themselves from the main group and were
attacking the stalled wagon. They fell back hastily before
the unnerving accurate fire of one man. McAllister noted
with surprise that the one man was Toller. The gambler,
with a gun in each hand, was using the cookwagon as
protection for himself and his horse, and each shot struck an
Apache or an Indian pony.

Ferguson, his work at the traces done, jumped for his
mount and swung up on the saddle. The trooper on the
cookwagon's driver's bench snapped the three remaining
mules into movement, starting out after the other wagons on
the double. Sergeant Ferguson and Toller swung out behind
the cookwagon to fend off another Apache attempt at it.

For a few seconds, it seemed that the wagon would make
it. Then the trooper driving it stiffened, went forward off his

seat, and fell to the ground behind the hoofs of the two rear mules, still clutching the reins in his dead hands. The mules panicked and swerved abruptly to one side. The wagon spun around crazily. Two side wheels ran into the humped body of a dead horse. The wagon bounced upward and teetered for a moment on two wheels. Then a further wrench from the terrified mules brought the wagon crashing down on its side, wheels spinning in air.

Ferguson took one disgusted look at the wrecked wagon, cursed, and motioned to Toller. The sergeant and the gambler raced their horses toward the boulders. Half of Chata's mounted force swung over to cut them off.

McAllister, seeing this, rallied five of his troopers and thundered back to join Ferguson and Toller. At the same time Millard Graff, whose wagon had been first to reach the boulders, poked his new Spencer repeating rifle out between two jutting rocks, and began slamming shots into Apache ponies. As troopers joined Graff with their carbines, the deadly hail from the boulders made a continuance of the attack too expensive for Chata. The Apaches whirled away toward the mouth of the canyon, pausing briefly on the way to snatch up their wounded, set fire to the cookwagon, and kill its three mules.

McAllister, Toller, Ferguson and the rest of the troopers reached the boulders seconds after the firing dwindled away. The sudden silence was shocking. Panting and lightheaded, McAllister sat down on the ground and leaned back against a high rock. It was not till then that he felt the burning pain in his right side. Glancing down, surprised, he saw his blue blouse wet with blood. Carefully unbuttoning the ripped blouse, he examined his wound. A bullet had gouged a chunk of flesh off his ribs, but hadn't gone in or broken bone. McAllister ripped a piece of cloth from his torn shirt and pressed it wadded against the wound to stop the bleeding.

Ferguson hurried over to him. McAllister leaned his head back against the rock, looking up at the sergeant with overbright eyes.

"Well, Sergeant? What's the damage?"

Ferguson squatted in front of him, taking off his hat to wipe his streaming face with his sleeve. His sleeve was bloodstained, leaving streaks of dull red on his face.

Ferguson looked at his sleeve, startled. It wasn't his own blood. "Six missing, sir."

Hard lines deepened in McAllister's face. "Wounded?"

Sergeant Ferguson shrugged. "At least half the men we've got left have something. Not enough to slow 'em down much, though. Except privates Crowley and Tech. Them two're in pretty bad shape."

"How bad?"

"Have to carry 'em in the wagons. Guess they can still handle a carbine if they have to. Tech's got a slug in his guts. Crowley's leg is broke just below the hip. And three other men'll have to ride the wagons, sir. We're short of mounts."

McAllister nodded, fighting off the numbness in his brain. "Sergeant, pass the word for every man to go easy on what's left in his canteen. There'll be no refills for . . ." He tried to think where he was going to get more water, now that their supply was smashed with the cookwagon down there. It took a few moments for his mind to begin working normally again. He stood up slowly, holding the wadded cloth against his torn side. When he spoke again, his voice had the old strength and snap behind it. "Sergeant, tell the men we'll be barricaded here till Colonel Foster shows up. That may mean three more days. Figure on that. Each man's water will have to last him that long. Any man who fails to ration himself accordingly will just have to do without till the colonel arrives."

"Yes, sir."

"And, Sergeant, I want five men up on the top of this hill, facing the other way. I don't think they can get at us in force from that direction, but there's no sense taking chances on Chata pulling another miracle. And see that every man is properly armed. Dole out extra ammunition from the wagons to everybody, Toller and Graff included."

A sudden thought struck McAllister. He glanced around quickly. "Sergeant, have you seen Remsberg?"

"No sir. He's among the missing, too."

The continuing sound of gunfire reached Jess Remsberg as blurred echoes, cushioned by the hills between him and the fighting, bouncing along the walls of the twisting canyon. Jess raced away from the sounds, pushing to their utmost Lobo and the riderless army bay, whose reins he held in one outstretched hand. When he reached a place where the canyon forked, Jess chose the way to his left, a route strewn with fist-sized stones, rising sharply between narrowing redrock walls. Here he was forced to let the horses slow to a cautious climb. He didn't want Lobo or the bay to turn an ankle on one of those stones and go lame on him inside these hills.

Jess had made his decision within seconds of seeing Chata's trap spring closed around McAllister's column. By the time those two Indian boys had driven the batch of ponies out of the canyon toward the Apaches who were on foot, Jess had estimated the number of warriors attacking McAllister. And knew what he was going to do. One more gun wasn't going to help the troopers much in that melee down there.

Circling around behind the attacking Apaches, he had caught a stampeding army bay whose rider had been shot out of the saddle in the first ambush volley. Then, while everyone's attention was centered on the point of battle, Jess had raced into the maze of canyons cutting through the range of hills and buttes.

The narrowing canyon rose to a break through a saw-toothed ridge. There Jess found a bowl-bottomed corridor that pierced all the way through the solid rock of the wall on his left. Dismounting, Jess led the two horses into the corridor. It was shaped like a tunnel without a roof, and its curved sides were high, arching six feet above Jess's head. He hoped he wasn't going to run into the blind end of a cliffside or a sheer drop at the other end. He was picking his

way now by guess and instinct. The last time he'd
penetrated these hills, when he located Chata's camp the
previous dusk, he'd come in from the other side. Coming
this way, he could only keep edging in the general direction
of the camp, hoping nothing would stop him.

The end of the rock corridor opened onto a shale-strewn
lip descending the side of a cliff. At the bottom, a wide arid
gulch, filled with mushroomlike stone towers three times
the height of a mounted man, stretched away to the side of a
mammoth red butte. Jess remembered seeing this gulch
beyond Chata's camp the evening before.

The loose shale made for a dangerous descent of the lip of
the cliff. It took Jess almost half an hour to get Lobo and the
army bay to the bottom. Realization of the time slipping
swiftly behind him strung Jess's nerves tight. There must be
an easier, faster route than this that Chata had used.

Jess mounted Lobo and pushed quickly across the floor of
the gulch, threading his way through the pillars of stone. He
could no longer hear any gunfire. What he hoped to do
depended on the fact that all of Chata's warriors were
outside the hills fighting McAllister's troopers. The Apache
camp would be guarded only by old men, very young boys
and squaws. But if Chata's warriors returned before he was
in and out of that camp . . .

It lacked less than an hour to sunset when Jess rounded
the red butte and looked down into a jungle of stone gouged
and carved by a river that had flowed through this place
before history. Though there was no sign of an Indian camp
in that deep-shadowed tangle, he knew he was less than a
few hundred yards from it. He took Lobo and the bay into a
dark shadow and ground-tied them. Pausing only long
enough to check his bearings with his memory of where the
camp lookouts were posted, he drew his knife from its
sheath and went ahead on foot.

Crouching low, moving without making a whisper of
sound, he kept to the long, dark shadows as he worked his
way down through a labyrinth of rock. Within five minutes
he spotted what he was looking for—a massive whitestone

arch with red streaking it like dripping rust. Bending lower, Jess made his way toward it behind the protection of a jumbled line of boulders. Where the boulders ended there was a growth of junipers. Jess slithered under them on his stomach, knife held ready. When he reached the limit of the bushes he was less than twenty feet from the great arch.

Jess lay still, scarcely breathing, squinting at the murky darkness under the arch. He saw nothing. He lay still and waited.

Minutes crept by. The small of his back began to itch intolerably. It required a distinct effort of will not to scratch it. Something moved in the deep shadow under the arch. A man stepped out into the tricky light, an ancient Indian, gnarled and wrinkled, a rifle cradled against his caved-in chest. For all the old man's painfully thin limbs and flabby paunch, there was pride in his bearing as he stood there in an attitude of listening.

Jess knew the old Apache couldn't have heard his approach. Perhaps he had sensed something wrong, or was only listening for the return of the warriors. Jess looked at the old man's sparse white hair. Then, careful to make no sound, Jess returned his knife to its sheath and lifted the Colt from his holster.

When the old man turned to re-enter the shadow under the arch, Jess came to his feet like an unbound spring. The old man turned awkwardly just as Jess reached him. The Indian fumbled with his rifle, opened his wrinkled lips to yell. Jess hit him carefully across the temple with the barrel of the Colt, caught him as he fell.

Quickly, he dragged the senseless old Apache to one side of the arch, lowered him gently. Then he went back, picked up the fallen rifle, and stepped into the shadow under the arch. From there he could look down at Chata's camp in the gully, see that things were as he'd seen them last time— except that there wasn't a warrior in sight. There were only the warriors' families to be seen among the temporary wickiups and small, almost smokeless, cookfires. Just below and to one side of the arch, where the gully bottom began to flatten out, were all the spare Apache ponies in a flimsy rope corral, guarded by an old man and two boys. Only the old man had a rifle. The boys had bows and arrows, and knives at their waists.

Silently, Jess left the shadow of the arch and made his way back toward his horses, pausing along the way to drop the ancient Apache's rifle behind some rocks.

The shadows were deepening fast, merging with each other in a prelude to total night, when Jess led Lobo and the bay to the whitestone arch. Keeping a good grip on the bay's reins, he mounted Lobo. Then he tied one end of rope to the bay's reins, looped the other end over his saddlehorn. Gathering Lobo's reins tight in his left hand, he raised his Colt in his right, thumbed back the hammer, and kicked Lobo sharply. The next instant he was racing through the arch and down into the gully.

He was through the arch before the first shout of alarm from up ahead. Jess swerved Lobo to one side and pounded straight-on at the rope corral, firing into the ponies and yelling madly at them.

The ponies began rearing, snorting with terror, milling about. The old Apache guarding the corral began clumsily levering a load into his rifle. An arrow from one of the boys whistled past Jess's ear. The next instant the ponies broke through the flimsy rope barrier in a wild rush that scattered their guards, and stampeded madly down through the gully.

Jess swung in among the rear ponies, harrying them on faster. They went into the Apache camp like a whirlwind, knocking over wickiups, trampling down fires, making people caught in their destroying path scramble aside for their lives.

Jess laced in and out through the confusion in the wrecked camp, yelling at the top of his lungs: "Mrs. Graff! Ellen Graff! Ellen Graff!"

An old man appeared suddenly in front of Jess, raising a carbine to fire. Lobo trampled him down, screaming. Jess snapped a shot with his Colt at a boy taking aim with bow and arrow. The shot missed, but the boy dropped his bow and threw himself aside.

"Ellen! Ellen Graff!"

She appeared abruptly, off to his left, from around the side of an askew wickiup. She stood there for a moment, stock-still, looking at him with shock gripping her face, her hair a wild tangle around her head and down to her shoulders. Jess swung over to her instantly, shouting: "Ellen! Mount up! Ellen!"

Recognition broke her shock as he neared her. She came running awkwardly to meet him. As he drew up beside her, he saw the screaming baby she clutched to her breast.

Jess holstered the Colt and reached down. "Gimme!"

She started to pull back, instinctively.

"He'll be safer with me!" Jess yelled at her. "Hurry!"

The certainty of his command caught her. She held up her baby. Jess snatched the boy up with one hand, held his squirming little body down hard across the saddle between him and the pommel.

An instant later Ellen was up on the army bay, racing away with Jess, back toward the arch. A scattering of shots followed them, but none close enough for accuracy. The stampeding ponies had cleared the way for the short time Jess had needed.

They went up through the arch and out into the mushroom-pillared gulch. Jess unfastened the lead rope to Ellen's bay and led the way without wasting time on talk. Ellen followed close behind as he headed along a torturous path into a canyon maze.

Jess had made up his mind that they couldn't get out of these hills the way he'd come in. That would be taking a chance on running into Chata and his returning warriors. Instead, Jess headed the other way, seeking the route by which he'd come into the hills from the other side the day before. Once out, he'd have to circle the hills and try to get to McAllister with Ellen and her baby before Chata found their trail and caught them.

But the total darkness of night closed in around them before he found the path he was seeking.

NINE

Jess had to crouch low to enter the snug little cave.

He went to his knees and crawled over to where Ellen sat before the dying cottonwood fire, drinking coffee from his tin cup. When Jess removed his hat and sat beside her, the top of his head was only inches from the rock overhang. The cave was nothing more than an open space under an outcrop of cliff rock, but it served its purpose. The fire couldn't be seen from outside it, and the little smoke that trickled out was invisible in the night darkness.

"Couldn't find any more wood nearby," he told her softly.

Ellen nodded. "We can manage without a fire for the rest of the night. Here." She held out the cup to him. It was still half full.

"Don't you want to finish it?" he asked her.

"I've had enough."

Jess took the cup and gulped the rest of the coffee. It was still warm. He gazed at Ellen's red-haired baby. The boy was sound asleep, bundled in the army blanket Jess had taken from behind the bay's saddle. He'd been soothed by a meal of sugared water warmed over the fire, and hardtack softened to mush from soaking in the water. Not much of a meal for a baby, but it had filled him and he'd fallen asleep on it.

"I didn't hear anything out there," Jess told Ellen.

"Did you expect to?"

"No. Not likely Chata'll try trailing us till sunup. Maybe not even then, if Gil McAllister's keeping him busy. But you never can tell. I've got the horses pegged down where they don't show against the stars. But if any of Chata's warriors were scouting around close by they could stumble on 'em by dumb luck."

Ellen shivered suddenly, and Jess realized that the dry chill of night was already penetrating the fire-warmed cave. He handed Ellen his own blanket.

"Here. Wrap this around you."

"How about you?"

"I'm more used to going without. And I'll be moving around a lot tonight."

Ellen's green eyes studied him as she drew the blanket around her. "You are worried about them coming up on us in the dark, aren't you."

"No. Just careful. You better get some sleep. It'll be a rough day on you tomorrow."

Her green eyes continued to study his face. For a while he stared into the embers of the fire and pretended not to notice, but finally it made him nervous. He turned his head and met her stare.

"Ain't much to look at," he said, uncomfortably.

"Jess Remsberg," she whispered, "you're a strange man."

"I been alone a lot. Gives a man queer ways."

She reached out and took hold of his hand. Before he realized what she was up to, she'd raised his hand to her lowered face and kissed it lightly. His hand jerked back as though scalded. He felt his face burning and saw that Ellen was blushing too, no longer looking at him, but at the last glow of the fire.

"What'd you do that for?" His whole arm was tingling.

"A way of saying thank you," she said. "Words don't come easy sometimes. You risked your life. You still do. It feels wrong, just saying thank you as though you'd only handed me up into a saddle or something."

"No need . . ." Jess stopped himself, knowing she had a right to feel grateful.

"How did you know I was in Chata's camp?"

"Followed you," he told her, finding it hard to get the words past his embarrassment. "Clear down into the Tres Castillos mountains. I saw you down there the morning Chata broke camp. Only I couldn't think of any way to get you out then, with Chata's fighters all around you."

He could no longer see her eyes in the deepening murk of the cave, but he saw she was looking at him again.

"I won't," she said softly, "be silly and ask why you went to all that trouble and into so much danger, for me."

"Guess you know," he said, and felt his embarrassment ebb away for no reason. "A woman that looks like you gets sure of herself real young in life."

When she didn't reply to that, Jess said, "You know, after I found Singing Sky killed, I never thought I'd . . . never again. I must be wrong in the head. When it does happen to me again, it's over a woman who already has a husband. Two husbands."

"Nachee is dead," she told him, still looking straight at him though he couldn't make out the expression on her face. "His horse fell and killed him."

"That still leaves one husband," Jess said.

"Millard doesn't want me back. He never will."

Jess felt his throat tighten at the sudden awareness of what they were both thinking. He said bluntly, "He's gonna want you back even less, when he sees you've got your kid with you. Nachee's kid."

"I know."

The silence grew between them after that. Until finally Jess said, "I been out here so long, mostly off by myself, I guess I don't think like a civilized man any more. But what I'm thinking is about what I told you once. This is a real big country. A man and a woman and a kid could easily find a place where they'd never run into anybody that knew 'em before."

He waited till he realized she wasn't going to say

anything to that. He felt heavy and clumsy as he cleared his throat and murmured, "Guess that was a pretty offensive thing for me to say. Just figure like I said; I'm not civilized any more. Forget I shot my mouth off."

He stared through the entrance of the cave at a small patch of stars glittering in the dark sky between two upthrusts of rock. He cursed himself for having spoken to her as though she were free. He wasn't free either, for that matter. Not till the man who killed Singing Sky had died.

"Jess."

Her voice made him turn his head towards her. He saw that she was holding the blanket open.

"There's room," she said softly. "It's a big blanket. No sense your having to spend the night shivering with the cold."

Lieutenant McAllister lay against the inner side of a boulder and squinted over its top at the dark mouth of the canyon in the first graying of dawn. His side was stiff and sore, the bandaged wound sending dull throbs of pain up into his arm and down through his hip. Sergeant Ferguson came up beside him, resting his carbine carefully atop the boulder between them.

"How're Tech and Crowley, Sergeant?"

"Not good, sir. Pain's got 'em both pretty much out of their heads."

McAllister nodded. "Colonel Foster will have Doctor Kuhn with his company. Tell them that. They'll just have to hold on this way till the colonel gets here."

"Yes, sir." Ferguson peered over the top of the boulder. "Any sign of Chata yet, sir?"

"Nothing." McAllister hesitated, then said quietly, "Sergeant, I want you to pass the word to the men. About the wagons. If I am . . . unable to give orders for any reason, and it becomes certain to whoever's left that we're going to be wiped out, I want those wagons burned. Don't alarm the men if you can help it, Sergeant. I don't think it's going to happen. But if it does, the ammunition in those wagons must not fall into Chata's hands. You understand?"

Ferguson cleared his throat and said, "Yes, sir." He picked up his carbine and slipped away.

McAllister regretted having to give that order. It could not fail to sound a note of doom for his men. But it couldn't be helped.

Actually, he didn't expect this command to be wiped out. They were in a good defensive position. His men were scattered among the rocks, where attacking Apaches would have only heads and arms to take aim at—while the attacking force would be open targets all the way to the rocks. The wagons were down out of sight in the depression between the boulders and the side of the hill behind them. Some of his men were up on top of that hill to watch for any Apache attempt to slip up on them from the other direction.

It was as well-barricaded a position as he could have found. All they had to do was stay here and hold it till Colonel Foster's troops arrived in force. He was sure Foster would arrive before their water gave out.

Sunlight abruptly flooded across the flat and smacked against the hills as the blood-red rim of the sun poked over the horizon. The light filled the canyon mouth. There wasn't an Apache to be seen in it. McAllister began to sweat with the waiting.

A man climbed up the boulder alongside McAllister. It was Toller. Up behind him came Millard Graff, settling on the other side of the lieutenant, resting his Spencer against the boulder.

"Good morning, Lieutenant," Toller said. There was a smile on his unshaven face, but it wasn't a real one.

"You sound as if you've been asleep," McAllister told him.

"Surprisingly enough, I did sleep. I was exhausted."

"You did a good job yesterday, Toller, helping Sergeant Ferguson try to save the wagon. That was damn gutsy work, and I intend to say so in my report."

The gambler smiled sardonically. "Life is most peculiar, Lieutenant. I must say, I never expected to end up being commended in a *Union* Army report."

"Well, you will be." McAllister turned his head to the freighter. "Graff, I understand you did some pretty expert work with that Spencer of yours."

"I hit what I shoot at," Millard Graff said flatly.

"I'm grateful you do."

"Don't be grateful to me," Graff told him angrily. "I'll tell you to your face, McAllister, I'm going to report you for this."

"Oh," McAllister murmured in a bored voice, focusing his attention back to the mouth of the canyon, "you're on that again. Save your fight for the Apaches."

"I don't mind killing Indians for you, McAllister," Graff snapped. "But I put out a hell of a lot of money for what's in my wagon. If I lose that wagon, it'll ruin me."

McAllister told him, "I hope you live to worry about it."

"I asked you for safe escort to Fort Duell for my wagon. If you aimed to go on an Apache hunt, it was your duty to warn me off, not drag my goods into it. You let me come along, not knowing. I've got some influence, McAllister. I'm going to lodge a complaint against you first thing we get to Fort Duell."

"Now that you've had your say," McAllister told him in a quiet voice that had a thin edge to it, "go pick yourself another rock and make yourself useful. I don't want to break your neck. I need every man I've got."

Graff opened his mouth to retort, but shut it without speaking and went away.

Toller commented, "You know, Lieutenant, the strange thing is that he really isn't angry with you because you've put his life in danger. He's furious because you put his business in danger."

McAllister nodded without answering. He could understand what was biting Graff better than Toller could. McAllister himself was not worried about losing his life out here. He was too concerned about the possibility of losing his military reputation. He had blindly led his troops into a trap. That could be justified only if he now managed to keep

Chata pinned here with him until Colonel Foster arrived to wipe out the Apache raiding band.

If Foster didn't arrive on time . . . McAllister put that thought out of his mind. Corporal Harrington would have delivered the dispatch to Colonel Foster by late yesterday evening, at the latest. Foster's company must be on its way by now.

"Lieutenant," Toller asked, "want me to bring you some coffee?"

"Had mine, earlier."

He watched Toller climb down the boulder and head for the wagons. Then he snapped his gaze back to the empty mouth of the canyon.

The sun rose higher. Its heat beat down, seeming to increase in weight with each passing hour. McAllister watched and waited, expecting at any moment to see Chata's warriors come howling out of that canyon toward him. There was no sight of an Apache, no sound of one. His nerves tightened unbearably.

The sun was directly overhead when McAllister knew he could wait no longer. A suspicion was growing in his mind that Chata had outwitted him again. The Chiricahua chief, having hit the troopers hard and pinned them out here, might have headed straight back to his camp, packed up the women and children, and headed north out of the hills last night. McAllister had a vision of waiting here till Foster arrived, and then going into the hills to find that Chata had left them and put several days' fast travel between his band and the army.

Sliding down from the boulder, McAllister called for Ferguson.

"Sergeant, you will be in command until I return."

"Return from where, sir?"

But McAllister was already shouting: "Logan! Fox! Gruber! Robertson! Brown!"

When the five troopers arrived from their positions in the rocks, McAllister told them quickly, "We're going to scout that canyon and locate the Apaches, if they're still there. If they are—" he glanced at Ferguson "—we'll need all the covering fire you can deliver to get back here safely."

"We'll cover you, sir. May I make a suggestion?"

"Go ahead. Unless it's that you want to take out this patrol in my place."

"That's what I had in mind, sir."

"I'm taking this patrol out, Sergeant. Just give us the best cover you can." McAllister turned away abruptly.

McAllister rode out in the lead. Behind him followed the five mounted troopers, each, like McAllister, carrying a carbine out and ready. McAllister tensed as he rode out of the protecting rocks, expecting the instant slap and whine of a shot, to feel the shock of it slamming into his body. There was only the deep, heavy silence. All that disturbed it was the clop of horses' hoofs and the creak of leather. McAllister was uncomfortably aware that he was sweating badly. The carbine felt slippery in his hand.

The six blue-uniformed men rode slowly, single file, toward the mouth of the canyon. It opened wider as they neared it. The craggy sides of its approaches loomed higher. McAllister noted how many places up the uneven, rocky rises might conceal Apache marksmen, felt sharply how big a target he made. He turned his head and glanced back at the boulders. They looked far away. The heads and carbine barrels of his troopers looked very small, and very few.

It happened then: the sharp crack of a rifle from the wall of the near approach to the canyon mouth. The first man behind McAllister, trooper Logan, doubled forward suddenly in his saddle, clutching desperately at the pommel to keep from falling off.

And then came howls McAllister had been expecting all day. Twenty mounted Apaches came pouring out of the canyon, firing as they charged.

That was all McAllister wanted to know. "Get back to those rocks!" he yelled, squeezing off a shot into the oncoming horde and wheeling his mount.

His patrol swerved back and tore for the boulders through a hail of lead. All except Logan. It was all Logan could do to hang on to his saddlehorn. His horse was jittering around, terrified amid the racket of gunnery, its reins dangling loose. McAllister spurred over, bent and grabbed the reins of Logan's horse, and raced towards the boulders dragging it along after him, hoping Logan could hang on.

He was halfway back when he jerked his head around and saw that he was leading a riderless horse. Dropping its reins, he applied himself to driving his mount the rest of the way to the boulders. He was almost up to them when his horse stumbled and went down hard, somersaulting over its broken neck. McAllister jerked his boots out of the stirrups at the first stumble, let go of the reins and hurled himself off and aside. He landed on his feet, tripped, caught his balance with a wrench of his body. He sprinted the rest of the way into the protection of the boulders with bullets kicking up spouts of dust all around him.

Throwing himself behind the first boulder he reached, McAllister instantly shoved himself up beside the man who was there, firing steadily over the top. It was Millard Graff, his face a mask of concentrated hate, his eyes seeming to bulge from their sockets. McAllister hauled himself up and squinted over the top of the boulder.

The Apaches had already turned back before the withering barrage from the boulders, and were racing away into the canyon mouth. They were about seven mounted men less than when they'd charged out of that canyon.

Sergeant Ferguson came dodging low through the boulders toward McAllister. McAllister slid down to meet him and sat on the ground, panting. Ferguson squatted in front of him.

"Gruber, Fox and Brown got back okay, sir. And you."

McAllister's eyes narrowed as though with pain. "Logan and Robertson. Both dead?"

Ferguson nodded. "I watched 'em a while. They ain't moving. And we lost three mounts. Robertson came back afoot, like you, sir."

McAllister rubbed the wet palms of his hands hard across

his face. "Well," he mumbled. "Now we know. Chata's still with us."

"Yeah. What I can't figure, sir, is why he didn't attack us before this."

"Why should he, Ferguson? He knows we lost our water with the cookwagon. Either the thirst will kill us, or we'll have to come out of these rocks and let him hit us in the open. What he doesn't know is that Colonel Foster is on his way with a full company."

"Yeah. So all we have to do is wait. That what we do now, sir? Wait and let him think he's got us, till the colonel shows up. Then we've got Chata."

The firing had dwindled to sporadic shots, troopers finishing off downed Indians that moved, Apache marksmen up on the sides of the canyon approaches trying to pick off troopers among the rocks.

"That's it, Sergeant." McAllister got to his feet, felt the wound in his side bleeding through the bandage. "All we have to do now is wait." All they *could* do now was wait, he thought.

Jess Remsberg had been riding south around the outer ring of hills all morning, Ellen riding beside him, carrying her baby up against her shoulder. It was when he judged that they were far enough south that he turned east through the foothills and saw the man up ahead.

He drew rein instantly, turning to Ellen and motioning her to a halt. He saw that she had already seen the man, too. Her face was ashen.

"He . . . is he . . ."

"Wait here. I'll be right back."

"What did . . ."

"Just stay here!" Jess growled. "Stay here. And look the other way, damn it!"

But she wouldn't turn her head, and he saw that she couldn't. At least she didn't go nearer. She stayed where she was while Jess rode forward alone.

The man was naked, spread-eagled face up on a short

space of salt-flat. Jess dismounted and went the last few yards on foot. The man's whole body had been burned. Not deeply. But every inch of skin below his neck had been burned off. Knives had done horrible things to that charred body. But again, not deeply enough to kill. He'd been alive when they'd staked him out here, to stare straight up at the burning sun. Little sharpened stakes on either side of his face made sure that he could not turn his head to evade the downthrust of those broiling sunrays. His eyelids had been cut off.

It was Corporal Harrington, the trooper McAllister had sent to Fort Duell to fetch Colonel Foster.

TEN

The rain struck suddenly, swiftly, an hour later as they
skirted the raw mud-colored side of a giant mesa. One
moment there were several gray-black clouds overhead,
drifting low across the hills. The next moment the air and
sky became hazy. Then the water came down in a rush,
striking with solid impact and the sound of a thousand
waterfalls.

Gasping, strangling, Jess and Ellen got their mounts over
against a mesa outcropping, where the water reached them
only in spatters thrown up when the rain bounded up off the
ground. The baby broke into loud wails, but Ellen,
shielding the child from the rain with her body, had him
soothed and quiet in a few minutes. And within ten minutes
the rain was over, shut off as abruptly as it had been turned
on.

The air cleared instantly, becoming even more brilliant
and dry-hot than before the deluge. Water rushed across the
earth in sheets and streams and was soaked off into the
sponge of the parched land faster than it could evaporate
toward the roasting sun. When Jess started out again with
Ellen the ground was barely damp. Soon the last of the
moisture was gone from the air and the land lay before them
bone-dry, hard and cracked. Their clothes were stiff with
baked-in dust and the salt of dried sweat. Anyone who had
slept through the rain would have had no way of knowing
now that it had rained at all.

They cleared the end of the mesa and rode east through the last scattering of foothills. Jess's eyes roamed the sides and crests of the hills ceaselessly. But part of his mind took no part in registering what he saw. He rode with troubled thoughts, turning the problem of the next few hours over and over. He found nothing but thorns no matter which way he studied it.

The sagebrush flat was in sight through the small buttes ahead when the baby began to wail again.

"He's hungry," Ellen said, riding close beside Jess. "Matter of fact, so am I."

Jess nodded, glanced at the surrounding ridges. "We can rest a while here." He dropped his canteen and saddlebags to the ground. "I'll have a look around."

Swinging Lobo away, Jess rode to the tallest nearby hill, drawing his carbine out of the boot as he reached it. He dismounted and led Lobo up the long, easy slope. On top of the hill he turned slowly, studying the folded, upthrust lay of the land around him. He saw no sign of Chiricahuas. Taking up his binoculars, he trained them on doubtful spots—breaks in ridges, shadowed folds of rock, a movement of dust-haze along their backtrail.

Satisfied at last, he rode back down to Ellen, who had already scooped a hole in the hard ground and started a small fire of bunchgrass in it. Over it she heated sugared water for her baby, and then coffee for themselves. Jess marveled at the way the boy went smack to sleep on the ground when he'd had his fill of mashed hardtack. A fed baby had no troubles on his mind.

Ellen and Jess sat close together after finishing their lean meal. Jess gazed at the flat beyond the buttes as he built a cigarette. He lit it and dragged in smoke, deep and slow, blew it out in a thin stream.

"Ellen," he said suddenly, "I've been studying what we've got to do next. There's only one thing I can think of."

"Whatever you say, Jess," Ellen told him quietly, resting her hand on his arm. The gesture of affection was done naturally, embarrassing neither of them though each was aware of its meaning, of the bond between them that it signified. A bond they had not discussed, whose future they had not explored.

"First," Jess said, "I thought about trying to take you and the boy straight on to Duell. We'd have a better chance of dodging Apaches by ourselves. I know a place on the way where there's water. Drink up and then fill both canteens, and I think we'd have enough to keep us going till we got to Duell." He dragged at the cigarette and met Ellen's green eyes. "That's the safest thing we could do. Only I just can't do it."

Ellen nodded, saying nothing. Jess looked away toward the flat and said, "The man we found dead back there was Corporal Harrington. He was supposed to get to Fort Duell and bring back reinforcements. He didn't make it. Gil— Lieutenant McAllister—doesn't know that. I know Gil and I know what he had in mind. I figure he's forted-up pretty near where Chata hit him, just trying to hold Chata with him till the troops come out from Duell to join him. He wouldn't try a finish fight with Chata. Chata outnumbered him two to one. Maybe more now, because I took Gil right into an ambush."

Jess dropped the butt of his cigarette and crushed it with the heel of his boot. "Whatever Gil's doing, it's with the idea that a lot more troops are gonna show up any minute. I've got to let him know they're not. You see?"

"Of course," Ellen told him. "Those troopers will all die if the lieutenant doesn't realize the situation he's in."

Jess nodded, dampened his dry lips with the tip of his tongue. "Ellen, there's something I didn't tell you. Your husband is with Gil."

Muscles in her face jumped. She lowered her eyes to her hands and looked at them dully. After a moment she said, "I can't see that that affects anything."

"No. It doesn't. I wish I could take you and the boy straight on to Duell, Ellen. I don't know how much of a force Gil has left. If we can manage to join his troopers, our chances of getting through ain't any better than theirs. And we've got no way of knowing what their chances are."

"They're better than my chances were before you took me out of Chata's camp, Jess. Chata was going to bury me alive in his son's grave."

"I've just got to do this, Ellen. I signed to scout for Gil. I've got to let him know Harrington didn't get to Duell."

Jess slipped his Colt out of its holster and held it in his hands, looking at Ellen. "You know how to use this?"

"Yes." Her voice was a whisper, as though she'd read his mind. "I can handle guns. My father taught me, from the time I was old enough to hold one and sight it."

"All right." Jess handed her the Colt. He noted with approval that she checked to make sure the hammer was against an empty chamber, and that the next chamber carried a load, before tucking the Colt into her belt.

"We'll have to dodge Chata to get to Gil, most likely," he told her flatly. "If you see we're not gonna make it, shoot yourself in the head. Make sure it's a finish shot. Don't let yourself get caught again by Chata."

Jess stood up stiffly and looked down at the sleeping baby. "You don't have to do anything to your boy, Ellen. Apaches love kids, and anyway they figure he's one of them. They won't hurt him."

Ellen took up her son gently, not waking him, and stood beside Jess. "I like your saying that," she told him softly. "Most people would say he's better off dead than being raised as a savage."

"Nobody's better off dead. Come on, we'd best get going."

They cut north through the foothills, Jess riding on ahead from time to time, seeing that their route lay clear before them. He grew more tense as they neared the area where Chata had ambushed the column, fending off fears of what they might find there.

The sun was low against the ridges when Jess heard the crackle of gunfire. He drew rein instantly, stopping Ellen with his hand. He waited for a moment, listening. It had been only a few faint shots that he had heard and they were not repeated. Jess waited, his spine rigid. A few minutes passed. Then the air carried the sound of a single shot from the distance up ahead. Jess listened a few minutes longer, but heard no more firing.

"Just sniping," he told Ellen softly. "That means it's like I figured. Gil's got himself forted up where Chata can't get at him easily enough to risk an all-out attack. Stick as close to me as you can from here on."

Jess swerved to the right and began edging them out of the foothills toward the flat. His face was taut as his wide gray eyes flicked from side to side, watching as they moved slowly on.

Another shot cracked up ahead, nearer now. Jess recognized the formations of rock coming into view, and swung towards a sudden, sharp rise in the land. When they were near the ridge, he motioned Ellen to stop. Swinging down from his saddle, he crawled the rest of the way up, taking his binoculars with him.

Just below the crest he paused, then carefully raised his head till he could see over and beyond it. There, less than a quarter of a mile away below him, lay the sandy stretch where Chata had sprung his ambush. Jess focused his binoculars. The sands sprang into view sharply. Jess moved the glasses slowly, over the still forms of dead horses and men, the charred remains of the smashed cookwagon. His nerves jumped when he saw that wagon. He moved the glasses again, scanning the canyon mouth, the sides of cliffs. Minutes went by without his spotting anything that moved. Then Jess saw something—a small, dark figure crouched on a high rock outcropping beside the canyon entrance. Sunlight glinted briefly on the rifle the small figure held.

Jess didn't waste time looking for more Apache snipers. He swung the binoculars to the butte on which he'd stood when Chata struck the column. Then he began searching the nearest hills and piles of rock, until he spotted the glints of carbine barrels and the blue arms and shoulders of troopers among the boulders at the base of a hill. He couldn't see the other three wagons, but at the top of the hill he caught sight of the uniforms of other troopers, bedded down in the rocks at its crest.

Jess lowered the glasses and scanned the lay of the land between him and those boulders with his naked eyes. He gave special attention to the mouth of that canyon. He and Ellen would have to pass it to get to the troopers. It was a matter of taking a route that would keep them as far away from that canyon as possible—and still not take so long that mounted warriors racing out of it could cut them off before they reached the boulders.

Backing on his hands and knees till he was well below the crest of the ridge, Jess got to his feet, hurried back to Lobo, and climbed back onto his saddle.

"I've got them spotted," he told Ellen, his voice strained and quiet. It was hard to keep his words calm, the way they had to be not to frighten her. "When we get around this hill, Chata's lookouts will see us. No help for that. If we try waiting till dark, those troopers'll take us for Apaches when we ride in, and fire on us."

"Mightn't they . . . even now? I mean shoot at us before they realize . . ."

"Gil wouldn't let anybody get that nervous with a trigger. He's got field glasses. And they'll have us in sight a long ways before we get within shooting range. That's the bad part. You'll have to ride as if you're trying to kill that horse under you. We've got to get to the troopers before the Apaches get to us. Come on, I'll show you."

He led the way down the hill and around its base. He halted them where she could see their goal and were still out of sight of the Apache lookouts near the canyon.

"There," he told her, pointing. "Those rocks there, against that hill. See where I'm pointing?"

"Yes," she whispered. "It looks far away."

"Don't think about that. Don't think about anything. Just

aim at those rocks and keep going hard as you can till you're in them. That's where Gil's forted."

She jerked her head in a frightened nod. He could see that she was working herself up. If he allowed her much more time, she'd be too tight with fear to make it. He looked at the baby she held against her shoulder. The boy was making little contented sounds of pleasure, his small chubby hands playing with strands of Ellen's red hair.

"Here," he said sharply, reaching out. "I'll take your boy."

For an instant, Ellen's grip on the baby tightened in an instinctive move of refusal.

"You'll need both hands to ride and hang on," he snapped harshly. "You'll both have more chance of getting through if I take him."

Her lips were trembling as she held out her son. Jess took him, expecting a cry of fright from the baby. But as Jess drew him close, the tiny boy looked up at his face uncertainly for a moment, then gave him a wide smile and reached out chubby arms for his neck. Jess hugged the baby close, tight against his chest with his left arm and hand. The boy wound his arms around Jess's neck and lowered his head to Jess's wide, bony shoulder. Jess felt his heart swell, and experienced a rush of emotion that shocked him.

He looked at Ellen. "Take that Colt and slap your horse with it," he told her quickly, his voice sharp and insistent. "Get him going fast as he can right off, and keep him that way. Kick him all the way to those rocks. Don't lose that Colt while you're at it. And remember to use it if you have to."

She said, "I will," but so softly he could hardly hear her.

"I'll be right behind you," he told her. "Don't look back. Okay." He drew a deep breath, gathered Lobo's reins tight in his lean right hand, and snapped: "Go!"

For a second, he thought she wasn't going to move. Then she slapped the barrel of his Colt against the bay's flanks at the same time that she drummed him hard with her heels. The bay took off with a leap, went racing wildly across the edge of the flat, its hoofs sending up spurts of dust as it ran. Jess kicked Lobo to a hard gallop and raced out after Ellen, stayed behind her by not letting Lobo out to his full stride.

They were halfway to the boulders when Jess heard the pound of horses and spine-twisting challenge of Apache screams off to his left. Glancing aside as Lobo pounded on, he saw about a dozen Chiricahua warriors riding hard out of the canyon at them, brandishing rifles. At the same time, guns cracked from the side of the canyon approach. Jess felt a breath of wind against the back of his head as a chance shot missed him by inches. He hugged Ellen's baby tighter, let Lobo out a notch, pulling up beside the wildly-running bay, between Ellen and the charging Apaches.

Then carbines began to blast from the boulders ahead. An Apache pony went down with a scream. Another lost its rider and veered suddenly, tangling with those pounding up behind it. The Apache charge broke against the solid wall of lead flung from the boulders. The mounted warriors pulled back, firing at Jess and Ellen. But their aim was thrown off by their urgent need to get away from the barrage flung from the boulders. The Apache marksmen up on the cliff were too far away for accurate shooting at targets moving so fast.

The bay carried Ellen in between two sharp-topped boulders. An instant later, Jess was behind their shelter, drawing Lobo to a sudden, trembling stop. As he swung out of his saddle, Ellen jumped down from the bay and ran over, snatched her baby from him, looked at the boy wildly.

"They didn't touch him," he told Ellen.

She sat down abruptly on the ground, clutching her baby close, her bowed shoulders shaking with her sobs. The baby began to wail shrilly.

Jess squatted in front of Ellen. "Here. You're scaring the kid, damn it!" He grabbed the baby from her, held him before his face and began whistling at him. The boy's crying stopped quickly, his eyes going wide as he stared at Jess's pursed lips. The baby reached out a tiny hand and stuck a finger in Jess's mouth, cutting off the whistle. When the finger withdrew, Jess whistled again, off key. The boy chortled and stuck his finger back in Jess's mouth.

McAllister came scrambling through the boulders to them, ducking low. He stopped and stared at Jess and the baby, dumbfounded. Then he looked at Ellen, recognized her, and something about his face softened.

He lowered himself to the ground and grinned at Jess. "Hello, Papa."

Jess blushed and said, "He's . . ."

McAllister said, "I know," and looked at Ellen. Then back to Jess. "Thought they'd got you, when you disappeared like that."

Jess lowered the baby to his knees and met McAllister's eyes flatly. "It was something I had to do, Gil. You holding it against me?"

"Hell, no. If I had a medal to spare, I'd give it to you. It's just that I didn't expect to see you again this side of eternity. You keep on this way, Jess, and you might die of old age yet."

Ellen edged over. "I'm all right now, Jess. Thank you." Jess gave her baby back to her.

"Cute little kid," McAllister said. "Sure don't look Apache to me."

Ellen bit her lip, and Jess's face tightened into an angry grimace.

McAllister flushed and stammered, "I didn't mean . . . anything at all bad by that, ma'am. I just . . ."

Ellen forced a smile. "That's all right, Lieutenant. I understand." Then she looked up suddenly, and her face paled.

Jess and McAllister turned their heads and saw Millard Graff standing there, his Spencer clutched tight in his thick fists, staring at Ellen and the baby as though he'd been poleaxed.

The eyes of husband and wife locked. Neither spoke. Jess stood up quietly and walked over to where Ellen had dropped his Colt. He picked it up, looked at it, looked at Graff, then slowly holstered it. Neither Ellen nor Graff noticed, but McAllister did. He stood up and watched Jess, while Jess looked at the man and woman staring silently at each other.

Graff licked his lips and tried to say something. It didn't come out, and for a moment Graff looked as if he was going to cry. Then he turned, almost stumbling, and walked away like a man defeated, down toward his wagon. There was a hard, dull shine to Ellen's eyes as she watched him go. Then, lips pressed tight, she gave her attention to the baby on her lap.

"Lieutenant," she said stiffly, not looking up, "I need some food for my son. Cooked hot meat, if you have it. And a knife to cut it up with."

"Sure . . . Sergeant Ferguson!"

Down by the freight wagon, Millard Graff squatted with his back to them, slowly reloading his Spencer with fumbling, awkward fingers.

ELEVEN

Jess motioned to McAllister, and they both moved back among the boulders till they reached a spot from which soft-spoken words would not reach the ears of the others. Jess sat with his back against rock, making sure this did not bring his head into view for any Apache sniper from the cliff, before stretching out his long legs on the ground before him. He studied the gathering dusk as McAllister lowered his solid bulk beside him.

"How many men've you got left, Gil?"

"Only nineteen, including you, Toller and Graff. But we've gouged Chata worse than that."

"How bad?"

"Well," McAllister admitted ruefully, "he's still got about twice as many men left as I do."

"And he's got you pinned here."

"Because I'm *letting* him pin me here. That keeps him here, too."

"Got any water left?"

"We lost the cookwagon with most of our water."

"I saw it."

"Then you know. I've kept a pretty tight rein on the men. We've still got enough in our canteens for at least another day, short rations."

Jess sighed, holding back his bad news, knowing what it would do to McAllister. "That's not much water, Gil."

"It's plenty to last us till Colonel Foster gets here with his

reinforcements. I kind of expected him today. But he's sure
to be here by some time tomorrow."

Jess told him then: "Foster isn't coming."

McAllister looked at him without expression, waiting to
hear the rest of it.

Jess squinted at the sun lowering behind the ridges.
"Your Corporal Harrington didn't make it to Fort Duell. I
found him dead, back on the other side of the hills."

"How?" McAllister muttered, more to himself than Jess.
"How could Chata have gotten Harrington? Chata's band
was far south when I sent Harrington out. He shouldn't have
come anywhere near Chata."

"My guess, Gil, is that he had real bad luck."

"How do you mean?"

"Apaches've been busting out of the reservation almost
every day, slipping south to join Chata. I figure Harrington
had the bad luck to run into some of them."

McAllister nodded, his eyes staring failure full in the
face. "Could be. But how do you explain him in those hills?
He wouldn't have been traveling anywhere near them."

Jess shrugged. "It's a hard thing to get in an Apache's
mind, Gil. They managed to take him alive. I'd say maybe
they decided to carry him with them to Chata, sort of like an
offering, to show how tough and smart they were. Whatever
happened to him, the main thing is he never got to Duell.
And Colonel Foster ain't about to show up and pull us out of
here."

"And," McAllister added bleakly, "we've got only
enough water left to last us another day." He glanced down
and saw that he had his hands locked together, thick fingers
interlaced so tight the knuckles showed white. "I wonder if
Chata knows Corporal Harrington was on his way to Duell
for help. There are Apaches that can read English. But
Harrington might have been able to get rid of my dispatch
before they grabbed him."

"Maybe. But Harrington was tortured before he died. I'd
say he probably told them everything they wanted to
know."

"So Chata knows I'm just sitting here on my fat behind waiting for reinforcements that aren't coming. All he has to do is wait and let our water run out; then thirst will do his job for him. And that's exactly what would have happened if you hadn't chanced on Harrington's body and gotten here to tell me about it."

McAllister cursed softly under his breath. When he had it over with, he looked up at Jess and snapped, "All right. Where's the nearest water, Jess? All the way to Apache Pass?"

Jess hunched forward, face furrowed, staring at the ground between his legs as though studying a map there. McAllister waited, watching him tensely.

"There's a blind canyon I found once," Jess said at last, "between here and Duell. Pretty much along the line we'd be going if we were headed for Duell, too. Got a seep in one wall, lets down a steady spring of fresh water. I guess it's still there. I've been trying to remember if there's any place closer. But if there is, I don't know about it."

McAllister came up quickly onto his heels, squatting, his body rigid. "How far is it from here?"

"If we start out when it gets dark, and push hard, we might make it a little after sun-up tomorrow."

McAllister stood up, crouching so his head wouldn't show above the boulders. "Be dark soon. You get ready." He strode away to his troopers.

Jess raised himself off the ground and went down to where a small fire burned beside one of the army wagons. Ellen was there, cooking slabs of meat.

Her son was crawling around happily on the ground by the fire, playing with stones. He looked up as Jess approached, smiled that wide, gap-toothed smile, stood up and tottered to meet Jess. The boy grabbed Jess's leg for support, clutching tightly. Jess patted his head affectionately and grinned at Ellen. She looked as if she'd been holding her face too stiff, but she hadn't been crying. Millard Graff wasn't in sight.

"He acts so happy," Jess said, "I guess he's had his meal already."

The stiffness of Ellen's face relaxed in a small smile. "He has. I shredded the meat for him and he stuffed himself. Poor little fellow was hungry."

"So'm I. That looks like fresh meat you're cooking."

"Yes. Cut off a dead horse. If you don't mind it tough, I'm making enough for both of us."

"Can't be too tough for me to eat. My belly button's stuck to my backbone."

He squatted beside her, watching the meat sizzle but listening to the low voices of McAllister and Ferguson and the movements of the troopers in the rocks.

Toller showed up beside the fire. The past couple of days hadn't done the gambler any good. Heat and sun seemed to have shrunk him within his clothes. But there was a steady, sure look to his eyes. He tipped his hat to Ellen and said to Jess, "I understand we're moving out."

"That's right."

Ellen looked quickly at Jess, then at her son playing in his lap.

"Any possibility," Toller asked, "that the Apaches might attack us in the dark?"

"Night or day, they fight when they feel like it. Only reason for going in the dark is it's cooler. We'll make better time. And we want to get to water before what we have gives out."

"Then we can expect to be hit from the moment we get out of these boulders."

"No way of telling what Chata'll do," Jess told him. "But I'd say we all sure better expect to get hit. And be ready for it." He gripped Ellen's shoulder gently and looked at the fire. "Ain't that meat about ready?"

They started out five minutes after full dark, with billions of stars just taking hold in the black bowl above, and before the moon came up. There was no shouted command. Ferguson rode back past the troopers, giving the word quietly.

There was the nervous coughing of men, the creak of leather, shuffle of hoofs, shaking of traces, squeak of wheels turning—and then they were moving out of the boulders together, with McAllister making sure each unit held to its part in the tight group.

The mounted troopers rode in two short columns, the three wagons between them. Graff's was the middle wagon, canvas having been raised tentlike above the cargo he was freighting. Under this tent, some of his cloth had been stretched out to form a bumpy mattress the width and length of the wagon. The two worst-wounded troopers lay under that tent in Graff's wagon—with Ellen, assigned to the wagon with her baby by McAllister, doing what she could to ease their suffering. Though Graff, driving the wagon, was near enough for her to have touched, neither Jess nor McAllister had yet heard a single word pass between them.

McAllister and Jess led the way, southeast from the hills, straight across the flat. McAllister set a sharp pace that he intended to keep up all night. The horses and mules were not likely to collapse before reaching their destination at that pace; but they were going to be sorely punished by it before the sun rose.

McAllister rode with an unremitting awareness of the weight of his command on his broad shoulders. Visions of fame and fears of what failure would do to his reputation had been stripped from his mind. He felt cleaner without them. He had only one purpose now: to deliver to Fort Duell those who survived with him. He jogged along, tall on his saddle, his head up, senses keenly alert, ready for a slashing attack from the surrounding darkness at any moment.

The men behind him were ready too, each over-aware of the noise they made hurrying out across this flat, of how easy it was going to be for the Apaches to locate and strike at them. Each mounted trooper rode with carbine in hand, finger ready against the trigger guard. The driver of each wagon carried his firearm across his lap, where he could seize it instantly. Inside Graff's wagon lay three loaded carbines, one apiece for Ellen and the two hurt troopers.

The stars filled the sky above. The moon rose and cast its ghostly gray light across the flat. No attack came. Men's nerves stretched with the lengthening hours, and still they hurried on unmolested. Around them spread the moon-filled night, silent and empty. Only, of course, it was not empty. The Apaches were there somewhere, unseen. Keeping pace with them.

From time to time, Jess left McAllister's side and rode off alone on Lobo, loping out in a great circle that eventually brought him back to McAllister. Jess was certain Chata's warriors were out there. But if they were near, they must be drawing back at his approach. He never saw any of them. Nor did he hear them at any time. It was as though they rode ghost ponies.

It got to be midnight, then an hour past. Jess galloped up ahead to scout a massive tangle of rock rising up moon-paled in their path. Nerves aquiver, he rode into the rock labyrinth and through it, his finger on the trigger of his carbine, ready to squeeze off a warning shot if he got jumped. There was nothing in those rocks but more rocks.

Jess rode back toward the hurrying troopers and wagons and swung up alongside McAllister.

"They're not in there, Gil," he said with quiet frustration. He began to wonder if the danger they were ready for really existed. He explored this thought anxiously as they skirted the tangle of rock and moved on across a barren salt flat.

He drew Lobo over against Gil's mount. "Hey, General. What do you think Chata's waiting for?"

"You're supposed to be the big Indian authority," McAllister snapped, the strain telling in his voice. "Why don't you figure it out."

"I'm trying to."

"Maybe," McAllister said, after a moment, "Chata is just letting us help defeat ourselves, letting us get tired with riding, letting us get our nerves all unstrung with worry. Waiting for us to soften ourselves for him."

"Maybe," Jess admitted dubiously.

"Or he might be holding off for dawn. Apaches don't have any ammunition to spare. He might want to be sure his men can see what they're shooting at."

"Chata's letting us take him a long way from the families he's got camped back in those hills."

"Why not? There's no one out here but us to bother 'em."

"Gil, maybe Chata ain't following us at all."

"I think he is."

Jess said thoughtfully, "If I was Chata, I'd be long gone the opposite way by now, north to the Mongollons. He'd be safe in those mountains before we could get reinforced at Duell and catch up with him."

"Really think that's what Chata's done?" It was obvious McAllister didn't think so.

"I don't know," Jess admitted. "Just trying to figure out reasons why he hasn't attacked by now. He doesn't stand to gain too much but dead warriors by tackling us, even if he licks us. Apaches usually stick to raiding lone settlers and unescorted travelers, giving the army a wide slip."

McAllister said, "I think Chata wants the ammunition in our wagons. I've got a feeling Harrington must have told them about that."

Jess nodded, more to himself than McAllister. "That's sure a point to think on. And there's another thing. If Chata wipes us out, it'll make him bigger with the Apaches than Victorio and Nana ever were. Not just Apaches, either. The kind of glory Chata'd get finishing us off would be real practical for him. Every damn hostile in the country would rush to join him. He could end up with maybe a thousand fighting men under him if he pulled it off."

"That," McAllister said, "is why I can't believe he'd let us get away this easy. He wants the ammunition and the glory."

"And another thing. He's an old, sick man, with nothing but hate keeping him going."

"Which brings us back to where we started," McAllister

muttered anxiously. "Why the hell hasn't he attacked us? We're out in the open and he outnumbers us."

"Like you said before, Gil. Maybe he's waiting for dawn."

McAllister sighed heavily. "We're talking a lot of maybes, Jess."

"Yeah," Jess said. "I know."

He rode along beside McAllister till he could stand the fidgeting of his nerves no longer. Without a word, he swung away on a backward circle that took him far behind the moving wagon train. He halted Lobo and took a long, searching look around him.

The whole expanse of the salt flat showed in the pallor of moonlight. There were no Apaches in sight. But that didn't mean much. Lone Apache scouts could be out there somewhere, keeping tabs for the main war party. A lone rider could stay far enough off so you couldn't spot him, and still be close enough to watch the big moving bulk made up of three wagons and two columns of troopers.

Jess's throat was tight and raspy. His dry tongue felt as if it were covered with sand. He wished he hadn't talked so much with McAllister. Thirst was bad enough without making it worse with needless talking.

Lowering himself from his saddle, Jess uncapped his canteen and put it to his cracked lips. He let a thin trickle of the hot water seep through his teeth to lie on his tongue for a moment before swallowing it. The swallowing hurt his throat. Untying his neckerchief and wadding it in his hand, he trickled a little more of the precious liquid onto it. He squeezed out the drops of water into Lobo's mouth, then wiped the dust from Lobo's nostrils with the damp cloth. It felt deliciously cool and damp when he retied it around his neck before easing back up into the saddle.

He trotted Lobo to catch up with the wagons. As he rode, he held the canteen to his ear and jiggled it, listening to the water left to him. There wasn't more than another mouthful in the canteen.

Sergeant Ferguson met him as he reached the wagons, saw him hanging his canteen on the pommel.

"Got much water left?" Ferguson asked him.

"Not much. How about you?"

"Same thing. A couple of the men don't have any. I told them they'll just have to suffer. They were warned about going easy on their drinking. Lieutenant says we'll be getting to that spring you know about around dawn. That right?"

"We should, at the rate we're going."

"Think we gave Chata the slip?"

"No," Jess told him. "I don't know what Chata's up to. But whatever it is, he hasn't lost us, not unless he wanted to."

Jess swung Lobo in between one column of troopers and the wagons, rode up beside the middle one.

He looked sideways at Millard Graff, who concentrated on the reins held in his hands and did not look Jess's way.

"How're things in your wagon, Graff?"

"Guess they're all right," Graff said stonily. "Why shouldn't they be?"

Jess shrugged and let Lobo ease back, pulled over behind the tail-gate and drew the canvas flap aside a bit with his hand.

Ellen's voice came from the darkness inside, quick and low: "Who is it?"

"Jess," he told her. "How're things in there?"

"They're both asleep. Crowley keeps moaning. But I think Tech is really in worse shape."

"Baby peaceful?"

"Sound asleep. Are the . . . Have you seen anything out there?"

"No sign of 'em. You ought to be getting some sleep yourself, Ellen."

"I can't."

Jess sighed and nodded. "I know. Try to relax."

He let the flap fall back in place, rode up past the wagons

and joined McAllister again. They rode side by side without speaking.

The night slipped slowly by with the miles they put behind them. Jess watched the lowering of the moon, and the way the brilliance of the stars began to dim.

"Soon be sunup," he said to McAllister.

"Are we near?"

"The way I remember it, we ought to be."

McAllister rode back to check personally on his troopers, speaking softly to them, each in turn, making sure they stayed alert, that none of them started dozing in the saddle. When he rode back up to Jess, there was a perceptible graying to the horizon. They jogged on together, tension mounting like a swelling bubble as the light of pre-dawn pushed its gray hand up into the black-velvet night sky.

When the dawn sunlight came washing across the salt flat, it revealed a line up ahead of them; a long, low hump blocking the plain. Within an hour, they were close enough to make it out clearly; the raw, broken-cliffed wall of a great red-brown mesa, its top fringed sparsely with green.

"That's where it is," Jess said to McAllister. "Can't see it from here, but there's a break in the bluff, almost dead ahead. It's narrow. Leads up over rocks, and down into the canyon. It ain't a big canyon. All boxed in. Seep's at the end of it."

McAllister was standing in his stirrups, turning his head to scan the limits of the salt flat around them. He settled back onto his saddle and wiped his sleeve across his eyes. In the harsh sunlight, already beginning to charge the air with heat, McAllister's beefy reddish face looked grimly haggard.

"Damn it, Jess! Still not an Apache anywhere."

Jess nodded, staring straight ahead at the bluffs they were approaching. "I figured sure Chata'd hit us with first light. If he's around here anywhere, I'm scared there's only one place he'd be, now."

"He's in that canyon we're headed for," McAllister said. "That what's in your mind, too?"

"Uh-huh."

"Well," McAllister stated flatly. "We'll soon know. Only the one way into that canyon?"

"One way. In or out."

They rode on. To their right, the land began a rise to a few scattered hills. But the way ahead was flat, hard land right up to the bluffs. As they drew nearer, what had seemed from the distance to be a slight vertical wrinkle in the red-brown cliff widened, showing itself as an opening.

Jess pointed it out to McAllister. "That's the entrance into the canyon."

"What's it like?"

"Narrow. Full of rocks and boulders."

The lines of McAllister's ruddy face dug themselves deeper. "All right. We'll have to try it. Can't go any further without water. When we're closer, Jess, you'll go in ahead of us and have a look."

Jess looked at McAllister, stiffened in his saddle and stared past him.

"Gil!"

But McAllister was already jerking himself around in his saddle, seeing the line of mounted Apaches emerging swiftly from behind one of the hills atop the rise to their right.

McAllister's shout was followed like an echo by Sergeant Ferguson's yells. Traces yanked as the drivers snapped out their whips. The wagon wheels began to spin faster. Within seconds, wagons and mounted troopers were surging toward the bluff. Apaches kept emerging from behind the hill, thundering down toward the wagons, howling madly and firing their rifles as they came. McAllister swung his mount back to the wagons, rallying his riders to the vulnerable side of the on-rattling wagons, leaving Jess to lead the way into the canyon.

Jess raced straight for the bluff, crouched low over his saddlehorn, eyes on the canyon entrance. Behind him and to his right he heard the crashing of guns increase, joined by screams and yells. But he did not turn his head to look.

He was little more than a hundred yards from the canyon mouth when he saw the glint of sun against metal among the dense piles of rocks inside it. He jerked on the reins, spinning Lobo around in midstride, waving his arm frantically and yelling back at McAllister.

Too late. The wagon train was already within range. Behind Jess, from the rocks in the canyon entrance, the roar of guns flamed out at the wagons and their escort. Jess saw a trooper fold out of his saddle and two army mounts go down with their riders. Then he was racing back toward the wagons.

TWELVE

McAllister was already swinging the wagons sharply to the left when Jess reached them.

"Get the wagons out of range!" McAllister yelled at Jess, and swung back to his cavalrymen.

Jess let Lobo out to full stride, caught up with the three wagons that were bouncing and jerking their way over uneven ground almost side by side, and led them toward a spot where the guns from the canyon could not reach them. Glancing back, he saw McAllister hurling his cavalrymen straight into the charging Apaches.

He grasped instantly what McAllister was trying to do. There weren't more than twenty-five Apaches in that mounted bunch. If the troopers could smash them into the ground, prevent them from joining or being joined by the rest of Chata's band in that canyon . . .

But the Apaches didn't hold still for that. Moments before the troopers slammed into them, the charging warriors broke and scattered—each swerving separately around the cavalrymen and racing past them in the direction of the fleeing wagons.

McAllister wheeled his troops instantly, splitting them into two salients—one led by him, the other by Sergeant Ferguson. The two salients fanned out aimed back at the wagons, slashing at Indians on either side as they came.

But seven or eight Apaches were already out ahead of the points of those salients, between the troopers and the wagons, and coming fast.

The wagons were now beyond range of the canyon mouth. Jess yelled to their drivers to halt and form into a closed barricade. Dropping back, he drew Lobo to a stop and snapped his carbine to his shoulder, sighting at the same time on the nearest Apache and squeezing the trigger. The shot spanged in his ear as the bullet drove the warrior backward off his pony. Jess levered as he arched the carbine toward the next Apache and took aim. His second shot missed. Jess dropped the sights an inch as he levered the next load into the chamber, fired again. The Apache's pony went down in midstride, somersaulted and slammed the ground hard, pinning its rider.

Jess swung Lobo back after the wagons. The drivers were maneuvering so that each wagon formed one side of a triangle. Lobo carried Jess inside that triangle just before it closed. Seconds later, Apaches were racing past, firing point-blank into the wagons.

With no time to dismount, Jess found himself shooting over the backs of Graff's freight horses. Three carbine barrels poked out from under the freight wagon's canvas hump and began firing almost simultaneously. The trooper handling one of the army weapons suddenly stood up straight, dropped his weapon, and pitched forward to the ground.

Chata's warriors were all around them the next moment, coming in from all sides with McAllister's cavalrymen on their heels. Jess, glancing at Millard Graff, noted that the man had one thing—courage. Graff stood beside his wagon, bracing himself against it, firing carefully at individual targets. A grin twisted his mouth; he seemed to be getting some kind of release from the battle.

McAllister's troopers were slashing in from two sides now, downing every moving thing between them and the wagons. If the Apaches had had any notion about seizing the wagons, they dropped it quickly, racing off in a long swing from the troopers and back toward the canyon. Three Apaches caught between the cavalrymen and the wagons tried to fight their way free. They didn't make it.

Some of the mounted troopers started off in pursuit of the
fleeing warriors. McAllister and Ferguson hauled them back
to the wagons. McAllister had no intention of being drawn
into range of the marksmen among those canyon rocks.

As soon as the firing stopped, Jess looked inside the
freight wagon. Ellen, her face pale and slack, sat with her
son held tight to her breast, a carbine still clutched in one of
her hands.

"All right?"

Ellen nodded slowly and looked at the two wounded
men. Crowley leaned back against the side of the wagon,
his face tight with pain, breathing hard. Tech still stretched
out, holding a carbine pointed under the canvas. He wasn't
moving.

"Dead?"

Crowley nodded.

Jess grimaced and let the flap drop back, pushed Lobo out
of the wagon triangle and swung down beside McAllister,
who stood there with Ferguson, scanning the corpses of
men and animals scattered between the wagons and the
bluff.

"We accounted for at least a dozen of 'em, sir," Ferguson said. "More likely about fifteen. Double the number of
ours they got."

Jess glanced toward a trooper who lay against a wagon
wheel, clutching his bleeding middle and moaning wildly.
He was not surprised to see Ellen emerge from the freight
wagon and hurry to the moaning man. Jess looked back to
McAllister. "Still doesn't sound like we got off too well."

"We didn't," McAllister said bleakly. "I've got exactly
eleven men still on their feet. How many men would you
say Chata had forted among those rocks in the canyon?"

Jess shrugged. "All I can do is guess. From the way they
were shooting, I'd say there were ten to fifteen men in those
rocks."

"So Chata has about twenty-five bucks left." McAllister's mouth tightened with grim satisfaction. "That means
we've cut him down to half the force he had when he came
across the border. That's something, anyway."

Jess started across the corpse-strewn flat, rubbing his knuckles absently against the stubble along his jawline. "You won't think it's much, Gil, tomorrow at this time. We'll all be dying of thirst by then."

Sergeant Ferguson cleared his throat and said to McAllister, "Excuse me, sir. But can't we try bustin' into that canyon? If we're goin' to die anyway, we might as well do it trying to get through to that water inside. Least that way we've got a chance."

McAllister glanced at Jess. Jess shook his head. "No chance at all. There ain't a clear way through the rocks in the canyon mouth for a hundred yards. You have to slow to a crawl to get through. The way Chata's got his men entrenched in those rocks, he could stand us off easy with half the force he's got."

"Chata knew this was the nearest water," McAllister muttered. "He must have known we were heading here as soon as he saw us start out."

"Sure he did," Jess agreed. "That's why he let us come this far, using up the last of our water on the way. And I'd bet my horse he won't attack us again. All he's got to do is stay where he is, keep us from getting at the water in there, and wait."

McAllister turned his head and stared toward the southeast. "We'll never get all the way to Duell with empty canteens, not with that stretch of desert to cross. Jess, where's the next place we could get water?"

"No place nearer than Fort Duell."

McAllister snapped his attention to the bluff facing them. "Could we get into the canyon by going up over the top of the mesa?"

Jess shook his head. "It can be done, sure. But we'd have to go slowly, climbing down into the canyon, not more'n one man at a time. Chata could pick off every one of us before we got to the bottom."

"How about at night?"

"Chata'd be expecting that. He's sure to light fires inside the canyon. It's not a big canyon. He could easy light up all the places we could climb down by."

McAllister continued to stare at the bluff, not saying anything for a while. He stood there motionless, like a great, rough-hewn boulder, squinting at the wind-worn walls of the mesa.

"Sergeant," he said at last, not looking at Ferguson, "take out a detail and bring in the bodies of our dead. We'll bury them here. Make sure you don't get within range of those guns in the canyon—even if it means leaving some of our men unburied."

"Yes, sir." Ferguson turned away, calling out the names of troopers.

McAllister went on staring at the bluff, eyes hooded, deep in thought.

Jess asked him, "Want me to stick by you, Gil?"

"Not right now, Jess. When I've got it figured out as far as I can, I'll talk to you about it."

"Okay. I'll go help with the burial detail." Jess took his carbine from Lobo's saddleboot, reloaded it, and carried it with him as he set out after Sergeant Ferguson and his troopers.

He was only a short way from the wagons when he spotted a man crumpled face-down beside a stand of cactus. The corpse wasn't dressed in army blue, but he wasn't an Indian, either.

A band tightened against Jess's chest as he approached the still figure in the black frock coat. Squatting beside the man, he saw that the back of his head was soggy with blood. Gently, Jess turned him over and gazed down at Toller's dead face. The gambler's wide-open eyes stared blankly up at the sky, his face frozen in a grimace of shock.

No, Jess thought to himself, nobody's better off dead.

They got the burial over with as quickly as possible, lowering the bodies into a shallow common grave, covering them with hard earth and a mound of rocks and stones. The sun was down on the horizon when the survivors stood with bared heads around the grave and listened to McAllister delivering the last brief words. "Man that is born of woman has but a little time . . ."

When it was over, Sergeant Ferguson asked McAllister quietly: "Sir, I've collected their canteens. There's a little water in most of them. Shall I divide it up among the rest of us?"

"Yes." McAllister motioned to Jess, started walking away from the wagons. Jess followed him.

When they were out of earshot of the others, McAllister turned and faced him. "Jess, I want you to go to Fort Duell and get help."

Jess stared at him, startled.

"I know it'll be rough, trying to get through," McAllister said. "We know how Chata works, by now. He must have scouts out here somewhere, keeping watch on us, ready to cut down any courier I send out. But if anybody can dodge and outrun 'em, it's you."

Jess nodded, his face troubled. "That's so, Gil. I was thinking about some other points. I don't have enough water to get me across that desert. And even if I did, by the time I got to Duell and brought Colonel Foster and his troopers back here—well, you're all gonna be dead of thirst by then, Gil."

"I hope not. Listen to what I've got in mind."

Jess listened. He'd always had respect for McAllister as a fighting man. But until now he hadn't suspected the resources of desperation-triggered cunning of which his friend was capable. For the first time, he began to believe that McAllister really did have a brilliant future as an officer ahead of him—if he survived the next few days.

"It just might work," Jess told him after he'd heard him out.

"Might is the word for it," McAllister said grimly. "I wish it were more certain than that, but it can't be. I wish I could think of something better. How about you?"

Jess shook his head.

"Then we'll have to try it this way. It better work. I'll give you Sergeant Ferguson, and pick the four best troopers I've got for you." McAllister looked up at the darkening sky. "It'll soon be time."

"Gil," Jess said softly, "keep an eye on Mrs. Graff and her kid, will you? Whatever happens, don't let Chata get his hands on her again."

McAllister stared at Jess and shook his head. "You've got no luck, friend, have you?"

"What does that mean?"

"You know what I mean. She's already married."

Jess's gray eyes were cold and blank as they met McAllister's stare. His mouth drew tight and thin.

McAllister shrugged unhappily. "All right. None of my business." He held out his hand. "Good luck, Jess. What happens to the rest of us depends on you now."

"I know." Jess shook McAllister's hand, hard. They both started back to the wagons. . . .

They moved out before the moon rose. There was no effort made to muffle the noise of plodding horses and rolling wagons. Chata's scouts were. bound to spot their movement anyway, even in this nearly total darkness. Even by this first faint starshine, the three wagons loomed as too big a bulk to be missed.

But Chata's scouts would be too far away to make out individual horses and riders in this darkness, against the bigger bulk of the wagons. It would be impossible for distant eyes to count the numbers of the riders. What was to be done next depended upon that.

To Jess's sharpened senses came the taste of dust, the smell of sweating horses, the sight of more stars emerging in the darkness above with each passing moment, the sounds of their going bouncing off the side of the mesa as, they drew nearer to it. Jess rode close to the wagons, between them and the bluff. So did Sergeant Ferguson and the four troopers close behind him. Jess peered through the darkness at the looming cliff and studied its changing shape as the wagon train came closer to its base. Soon they were skirting the mesa, hugging its side, heading away from the canyon.

Then Jess saw what he was looking for, up ahead—a cluster of massive boulders sprawling out from the base of the bluff. Jess stiffened. Bending low over the pommel, he eased down out of the saddle, and kept on at the same pace afoot, leading Lobo. Glancing back, he saw that Ferguson and the four troopers were also afoot now, marching quickly alongside their mounts. But not leading them. Their mounts were linked by short lengths of rope. A mounted trooper tugged the lead rope tied to the reins of the first one.

The wagon train detoured around the boulders and kept going, pointing away from the mesa now, heading north-west, picking up speed quickly. To Chata's scouts, watching from afar as they followed, nothing about the vague shape of the wagon train seemed changed. But it was. Jess, Sergeant Ferguson and four troopers were no longer part of it.

Deep among the boulders at the base of the bluff, Jess and the five others watched the darkness swallow the wagon train. Then, tugging Lobo along, Jess led them down into a small depression between two boulders leaning against the cliff. Jess was the only one with a horse. The troopers' mounts were with the vanished wagon train. Even so, the area between the two boulders was barely big enough to hold them. But it was deep enough so that they would be completely concealed there, even when the moon rose.

Jess settled himself on the hard ground to wait. The others followed his example. No one spoke. Their breathing began to seem unusually loud to Jess, but he knew it wasn't—it was only fear and anxiety that made it seem so. Somehow, he felt, Ellen would be safer if he'd been able to stick with her instead of staying behind like this. There was no logic to that, but the feeling persisted.

McAllister, riding swiftly at the head of the wagons, did not look back. Yet his thoughts were behind him, with Jess, with Ferguson and the four troopers detailed to him—half his effective fighting force crouched at the base of that mesa, waiting, left further behind with every moving minute.

Much of the plan McAllister had formed depended on the fact that Chata was not likely to start following them right away. Not by dark. He'd wait until he was certain McAllister had given up hope of storming the canyon to get at the water. Chata knew there was no other water between that canyon and Fort Duell. He might even figure on waiting till dawn, sure his faster ponies would catch the troops and wagons easily before noon, thirst having slowed mounts and men down considerably by then.

McAllister intended to follow the route he was traveling for several hours. Then, suddenly, he would change direction and strike—straight and fast—towards the hills where Chata had first ambushed him.

Chata would come then. He'd come when his scouts raced back with the news that McAllister was speeding toward those hills. For the women and children of the Chiricahua band were in those hills, waiting in Chata's unprotected camp. Chata would come out after McAllister when he learned that; come fast, and in force, ready to fight. Only before Chata caught up with the wagon train, McAllister would have changed direction again—following a wide circle and then beginning a headlong dash straight back toward the canyon that contained water.

McAllister prayed that the darkness of night, and his many shifts in direction, would confuse Chata just long enough to give the wagon train a head start in the race back to that canyon. Whether they got into the canyon or not would depend on the men McAllister had left behind at the mesa.

It was Jess's job to lead Sergeant Ferguson and his four men up over the top of the mesa, and down into the rear of the canyon. Jess would start as soon as he heard Chata take his band out of the canyon in pursuit of McAllister. There was no way of knowing whether Chata would leave any men behind to guard the entrance to the canyon. But he couldn't leave many if he hoped to fight McAllister's troopers. And if any warriors were left behind, it would be with the thought of standing off McAllister, should he manage to swing back before Chata. They wouldn't be expecting an infiltration from the rear.

McAllister was forced to admit to himself again, as he rode along, that the plan was full of "maybes." But it gave them at least a fifty-fifty chance. Which was more than they'd have had trying to storm the canyon, or sitting outside it letting thirst do its work.

With Ferguson and his four troopers in the rocks, controlling the entrance of the canyon, it might work. Even if Chata caught the wagon train before it got into the canyon, it would be an open, running fight. Chata's warriors would no longer be forted up in the rocks, where they couldn't be seen to be shot at. And once they reached the canyon, the guns of Ferguson and his men would come into play.

The drawback was that if the wagon train *did* manage to get into that canyon, McAllister's force would be trapped in it. They'd have water, but no way to get out. By the time McAllister's force got to the water in the canyon, filled the canteens and allowed the horses and mules to drink, Chata's warriors would be ready outside the canyon, blocking their exit.

It would be only a question of how long McAllister and his men could hold out before Chata's superior numbers overwhelmed them.

And how long it would take Jess—who was to get going as soon as Ferguson had control of the canyon mouth—to reach Fort Duell and bring back reinforcements.

THIRTEEN

Sergeant Ferguson's hand reached out, found Jess's arm and pressed it lightly. Jess nodded automatically, before he realized that Ferguson could not see the nod in the pitch-black darkness between the two boulders.

"I hear it," Jess whispered.

It was the thunder of horses, many of them. Jess detected the tremor of the ground under him as he listened. Taking off his wide-brimmed hat, he shoved himself up, hugging one boulder so that he remained merged with its shadow. Rising on his toes, he could just barely see over the tops of the other boulders. What he saw was the merged, dark shapes of horses and riders, racing ghostlike across the moon-drenched flat going off to the northwest, the way the wagons and McAllister's escorting troops had gone, three hours earlier. The first part of McAllister's plan had worked.

Jess sat down again, settling the battered Stetson back on his head. He felt how taut he was, but made no effort to relax.

Ferguson whispered close to his ear, "How many were they?"

"Couldn't count 'em. A lot. If Chata left anybody in the canyon, he didn't leave many, that's for sure."

"I'll sure as hell hate myself for all the climbing we're going to do," Ferguson said, "if it turns out there ain't no Apaches guarding the canyon mouth at all."

"No you won't. You'll be damn glad. And you'll be alive

a little longer." Jess leaned back against the base of the cliff
and listened to the massed hoofbeats diminishing in the
distance. After a while, the sound was gone. All he could
hear was the faint whisper of the dust-laden wind, bringing
an elusive fragrance of sage with it.

He stood again, gazing out across the empty flat. Moving
to Lobo, he made sure the short length of rope hitching the
dun to a boulder was secure. Patting Lobo's neck gently, he
said softly over his shoulder, "All right. Time to get
started."

Leaving Lobo, Jess started out through the boulders,
feeling his way along, keeping his head down. At the edge
of the boulders he got in close against the base of the bluff,
into its dense shadow. Turning, he whispered to the others,
"Follow me single file from here on. Move as I do. Keep in
the shadows. Figure the first man that makes any noise is
likely to get us all killed. Be especially careful you don't
strike your carbines against rock." Then he moved onward.

Half an hour later, he reached the beginning of a narrow
shelf slanting upward on the face of the cliff. Slinging his
carbine over his shoulder, Jess started up it, hearing the
scuff of boots against stone as the others followed. Halfway
up the side, the shelf ended abruptly.

Jess reached up for the jut of rock he remembered, and
found it. Getting a firm grip with his fingers and shoving
upwards with his toes, he wrenched himself up onto the jut.
From there on it was all that way—muscle-stretching, lung-
burning work. Climbing by hand-holds and toe-holds barely
seen. Moving upward by precarious feel or brute strength.

It was slow, heart-twisting work. The night-shrouded
ground below began to seem a long way down. The top
seemed to keep retreating before their advance. Jess moved
up only a couple of feet at a time, waiting then till the
others, following along the way he'd shown them, reached
his heels and could see what he did next.

They reached the top two hours after starting the ascent.

Jess stretched out full-length on his stomach, dragging air
into his tortured lungs. Ferguson and the others flung

themselves down beside him, panting too hard to speak.
When he had his breathing back under control, Jess took up
the canteen strapped to his belt, uncapped it, and raised it to
his mouth. He got about ten drops of water, and that was all
there was. He capped the canteen, letting the water remain
on his tongue. There wasn't enough to swallow. It seemed
to just disappear in his dry mouth.

"Okay," he croaked softly. "Let's go."

He stood up and moved off across the top of the mesa,
crouching low to keep within the shadows. The others
followed, crouched as he was. From below, the top of the
mesa had looked flat. It wasn't. It was composed of a
tangled series of hollows, ridges and dips, sparsely grown
with saguaro, bunchgrass and brush. It afforded good
concealment, belts of deeper darkness in the night, that
stayed with them all the way to the inner rim of the canyon.

Motioning the others to drop down behind him, Jess
squatted at the edge and stared down into its blackness.

He saw nothing but the dark void below him. A whole
army could have been waiting on the floor of that chasm and
he wouldn't have seen it.

Jess began prowling the rim, seeking the way down that
he remembered. At last he spotted the landmark he
sought—a group of slender stone pillars like dark fingers
pointing at the stars. Jess quickened his pace as he neared
the dark fingers—then stopped abruptly. There had been a
stretch of flat ground between the stone pillars and the lip of
the canyon. That stretch was gone. Now the rear wall of the
canyon dropped away inches from the pillars. Jess crouched
low and peered over the side. Where once there had been
outcroppings, there was now a sheer drop into the darkness
below.

Sometime in the two years since he'd been here, this part
of the rear canyon wall had caved in. The descent no longer
existed. Not here, anyway.

Saying nothing to the others, Jess kept going along the
rim of the canyon, moving slowly, stopping every few steps
to strain for a look at what lay below.

Time sped past as they continued their snail's pace. Behind him, Jess heard only the soft shuffle of boots. They said nothing, not even in whispers, but Jess felt their increasing nervousness and impatience building up at his back like a solid weight. Time meant everything now. There was no telling when Chata would come racing back with his warriors, chasing the wagon train or even ahead of it. With each passing minute, the time when it would certainly happen drew nearer. They must be down among those rocks, in control of the canyon mouth, when it happened.

But there was no way of hurrying. Trying to spot some way down in the dark was tedious, frustrating work. But something rasped worse—the possibility that there was no other way down.

When, finally, Jess knelt and looked over the lip and saw shadowy juts of rock below him, his hands trembled with released tension. There was no time to try it alone and make sure the rocks did not give way, a few yards down in the darkness, to a sheer drop. He could only hope it didn't—hope with an intensity that made it a prayer.

Jess led the way, climbing carefully down the outcroppings with the others close behind him. Halfway down, the rock hand-holds did end. But Jess, feeling the way with his feet, found that the canyon wall did not fall away sheer below that point. Instead, there was an incline. A steep incline, but one that could, with utmost caution, serve as a way down.

The going after that became agonizingly slow. One slip, and a man would go rocketing down that steep slope in a fall that would gain terrible momentum before the floor of the canyon came up and slammed into him.

To Jess's ears their slow, clumsy descent made a tremendous racket. Boots rasped against the inclined wall, fighting for a solid hold. Small stones were dislodged, rattled down the slope to the rocky bottom. If any Apaches happened to be back in this part of the small canyon, Jess knew, he wouldn't be alive two seconds after reaching the bottom. He could only hope that any guards Chata had left behind were all at the canyon mouth—and that the noise of their descent wasn't carrying that far.

Jess reached the floor of the canyon and sat down immediately. His knees were shaky, his legs weak. One by one, the others came down beside him and dropped to the ground. They were all panting from the exertion and fear of the climb.

"We were lucky," Jess whispered when they were close around him. "That was a lot of noise we made. From here on, we can't afford to make any sound at all. Stick close enough behind me to touch me."

Jess looked up at the sky, saw the dimming of the stars. "Close to dawn," he said, worried. "Ferguson?"

"Yeah?"

"When we get there, we won't be able to say anything. So let's get everything straight now. When I touch your shoulder, you do the same to the man behind you and let it get passed on. That means I figure we're right on top of them. Drop down on your bellies then, and have your handguns ready. I'll move in on 'em, stir 'em up. It'll be lighter by then. Bein' low, you'll be able to see them when they pop us. Just remember I'm wearing this big hat. Don't anybody get so scared they shoot me."

"Let's go," Ferguson whispered impatiently.

Crouched low, Jess set off through the canyon, taking advantage of the deepest belts of darkness. He got in close to the inner wall of the canyon and followed its irregular curve. It didn't take long. The canyon was small. But by the time he sighted the dark shapes of the rock piles in the narrow canyon entrance, the sky beyond the canyon mouth was beginning to gray.

Jess dropped to his knees, glanced back to make sure the others did the same. Then he began crawling forward. Though the graying sky outlined the piles of rocks sharply by now, it was still inky-black down on the floor of the canyon. Crawling in that darkness, the six men were invisible. When Jess was in the canyon entrance, close enough to the rocks to touch them, he stopped, reached back, and gripped Ferguson's unseen shoulder briefly.

He waited, giving them time to pass back the signal, to get their army Colts in hand, and lower to their bellies. He was sweating heavily as he drew his wide-bladed knife from its sheath, and crawled between two jagged rocks toward the place where the canyon opened into the flat.

Holding his breath, Jess inched his way forward through the rocks. A voice dead ahead froze him. It was not an alarm. Just the voice of a man in conversational talk—Chiricahua Apache talk. Another Apache's voice answered the first one. Jess got his fingers tighter around the haft of his knife and inched toward the voices.

He froze again. In front of him, less than a foot away, suddenly appeared the high-moccasined legs of an Indian, darkly outlined against the graying sky. Quickly, Jess raised his head. The Apache had his back to him and was speaking to someone unseen.

Jess braced his legs, sucked air into his lungs, and drove upwards. One hand sank the knife deep into the Apache's back, the other hand whipping around against the Apache's mouth to shut off any outcry. The Indian spasmed in Jess's arms, breath whistling against Jess's palm. Then he crumpled. As he fell, Jess shoved him away with his knee, yanking his knife out of the dead man's back. Hot, sticky wetness streamed back from the blade over Jess's fingers.

As the dead Apache sprawled down among the rocks, another leaped up, yelling wildly. Jess sprang at him, knife held low. The Apache jumped backwards, momentarily out of reach, still yelling. Other dark figures suddenly rose up from the rocks. Behind Jess came the roar of guns, reverberating like cannons against the canyon's narrow entrance walls. Then there were screams, howls and more shots.

The retreating Apache halted, then came leaping forward at Jess. Jess saw the pale gleam of a blade in the Apache's hand, threw himself down on his knees, ducking low. The charging Apache's legs slammed into Jess's side. The

Apache went flying heavily over Jess's back. Jess twisted around with a jerk, grabbed for and caught the fallen warrior's wrist, and drove his own knife into the Apache's bicep. The Apache screamed as his knife clattered to the stony ground, clawed for Jess's eyes with the fingers of his free hand. Jess lashed his knife upwards, felt it rip into flesh, hit bone. He jerked it out, drove it in again. This time it struck no bone, sank in to the hilt. The Apache sprawled over on his back with a small sigh, and lay still.

Jess, crouched over him, catching his breath, suddenly became aware that it was already over. The shots, screams and grunts had ended that quickly. Getting his shaky legs under him, he stood up.

A gun flamed, yards away. Jess heard the roar of the shot as lead struck high rock behind him. A shower of tiny stone chips cut painfully against the back of his head and neck. He dropped back down, on his stomach, cursing silently. Then he realized that he had lost his hat in the knife fight. Feeling around the dead Apache's body till he found it, he settled it back on his head.

"Remsberg?" That was Ferguson's voice.

"Here I am. I'm standing up. Don't try to shoot me again."

Jess rose as Ferguson hurried over. Jess saw the four troopers behind him.

"Got every one of 'em," Ferguson exulted.

"How many were there?"

"How many did you take care of?"

"Two."

"Then there were eight of 'em," Ferguson told him. "Where the hell's the water?"

"This way." Jess led them back through the canyon, walking fast. The graying of pre-dawn was spreading through the sky too fast.

In the back wall of the canyon, just above their heads, water seeped out of a long crack in the rock wall, trickled down to the ground. There they found a wide pool of water, enclosed in a surprisingly lush growth of high grass and flowering bushes.

Throwing himself down at the pool's edge with the others, Jess drank greedily. The water was a miracle of cold wetness, washing fresh life and strength into him. He pulled himself away from the water and stood up while the others still gorged themselves on it. Leaving them there, he hurried out of the canyon and along the bluff to where he had left Lobo.

Before he reached the boulders, Jess stopped abruptly, feeling something. He stood motionless, absorbing the slight tremor of the hard ground under his boots. He held his head high, eyes straining. The light was too murky and uncertain for him to make out anything at a distance.

He was sprinting, ignoring his limp, when he reached the boulders. Unhitching Lobo, he rode the dun horse swiftly back to the canyon and led him through the entrance toward the water. Sergeant Ferguson and his four troopers were already in the rocks, each having chosen a secure spot and laid out his carbine, ready to hand.

"I think they're coming," Jess told Ferguson as he led Lobo in.

"The lieutenant? Or Chata?"

"I don't know."

Jess led Lobo to the pool. The dun lowered his head instantly, began lapping up the cold water noisily. Jess let the dun keep at it for only a dozen seconds, pulled him back from the water before he'd drunk his fill. He didn't want Lobo to get so waterlogged it would slow him down. Quickly, Jess filled his canteen.

As he led Lobo back into the narrow canyon mouth, Ferguson called out from the rock barricade, "I hear 'em."

Jess did, too. The faint sound of running horses was carried on the increasing wind.

"Good luck to you," Jess said to the troopers.

They waved to him and managed grins.

Ferguson called, "Luck to you. You can get drunk on me, if I get back to Duell in one piece."

Outside the canyon, the first rose glow of dawn was spreading across the salt flat. Off in the distance to the northwest, a cloud of moving dust rose high off the ground. McAllister—or Chata? Jess got a boot toe into the stirrup, swung up onto his saddle.

Three Chiricahua warriors appeared around the bluff, pushing their ponies toward the canyon. Chata must have sent them on from his main force, as soon as he'd realized he was being tricked, to alert those he'd left behind in the canyon.

They saw Jess as he saw them, yelled, and came on with an increased burst of speed from their ponies, raising their rifles. Jeff reined Lobo around and shot off in the opposite direction, across the flat.

He bent low over his saddlehorn, forcing Lobo to run as he'd never run before, hearing behind him the pursuing hoofbeats and shots as bullets fanned the air and spurted dust all around him.

The three wagons bucketed along, going so fast they reared and bounded dangerously each time a wheel slammed over a small stone or slight ridge in the ground. Whips cracked incessantly against the backs and over the ears of the animals pulling the wagons, forcing them to keep at their killing speed despite the drain of exhaustion and thirst on their strength. They would never be fit to run again; perhaps not even to stand. But to the men forcing them to race their lives out, all that mattered was that they last till they reached the canyon in that mesa in the distance.

McAllister and the four mounted troopers with him raced behind the wagons, glancing back fearfully from time to time. McAllister was so taut that he felt he was going to explode any moment. His luck had held too well, too long. It had to end any moment now. He knew it couldn't hold till they were safe inside that canyon.

It didn't.

McAllister saw the dust first, coming up over a rise in the

land a mile away to his right. Moments later the Apaches appeared, racing up over the rise.

Yelling to his four mounted troopers to follow, McAllister spurred his horse to an added burst of speed, galloped up alongside the wagons, between them and the Apaches. There was no need to shout anything to Graff and his two army muleskinners. They had already seen. Their long bullhide whips cracked out again and again. McAllister prayed that none of the poor animals dragging the wagons would die right then and there, before reaching the canyon.

Chata and his warriors were all over the rise now, thundering on in a pell-mell mass. Twenty of them, McAllister estimated quickly. Too many. Riding hard, keeping his mount alongside the wagons, he squinted at the mesa ahead. Two miles to go, he guessed, as he drew his carbine from its scabbard. Two miles. Only speed would save them now, not guns. Besides himself, he could bring only eight guns against those twenty Chiricahuas— including Ellen Graff and the three men handling the wagons.

Beside him, the lead army wagon suddenly hit a sharp rise and careened upward, balancing precariously on two wheels as it lurched on. For a split second, the wagon was dragged along teetering that way, ready to crash over on its side. Then it came crashing down on all four wheels again, shook itself like a live thing, and rattled onward.

Then McAllister saw something that made his heart twist with a new hope.

Chata and his warriors were not racing straight for the wagons any longer. Instead, McAllister saw, they were aiming directly toward the canyon along a converging line. This way, the two opposing forces wouldn't meet till they both reached the canyon mouth.

It was obvious what Chata had in mind. If he struck directly at the wagons, he could certainly reach them before they got to the canyon. And Chata's force could not fail to overwhelm McAllister's tiny band. But it would be a costly victory. Fighting with the wagons as protection, McAllister's men would take their toll before they went down.

Chata saw no need to waste any more of his band. All he had to do was get to the canyon first, fort his warriors among the rocks there, and stand off McAllister. They would be back where they started: if McAllister's force charged the canyon mouth, it would be wiped out by warriors hidden among the rocks. If McAllister did not charge, his force wouldn't last out another day without water.

The thing Chata did not know, McAllister realized, was that Sergeant Ferguson, with his four troopers, was now in control of that canyon entrance. Or was he? The doubt tore at McAllister as the two forces raced onward toward the looming bluff, converging on the canyon.

The wagons were too slow. Even driven as madly as this, they could not cover the ground with the speed of those racing Indian ponies. And McAllister and his four mounted troopers were forced to keep pace with the wagons. Chata and his warriors drew ahead steadily. Half a mile from the canyon mouth, the Apaches were up ahead of the wagons, increasing their lead with every pound of their ponies' hoofs.

McAllister swung his arm in a signal to the mounted troopers behind him, and spurred his horse on ahead of the wagons. As his four cavalrymen thundered up with him, leading the wagons toward the canyon, McAllister slid his carbine back in its scabbard, drew out his army Colt and cocked it. Watching the Apaches ahead closing in on the canyon mouth, he knew the clash was only moments away. When it came, it would be close action. Whatever happened, McAllister thought, he hoped he got a glimpse of Chata himself among those warriors—just long enough to level his sights on the Chiricahua chief.

The crashing of shots from up ahead bit through the clatter of wagon wheels and thud of hoofs.

McAllister saw the Apache band abruptly slow their rush at the canyon mouth. The crackle of guns continued. The

Apaches stopped, suddenly began to sag back and scatter, yelling. From the rocks in the canyon, shots blasted out at them steadily, cutting down ponies and Apaches. A wild shout of joy welled up in McAllister's chest, but came out of his parched throat only as a rasping croak. Raising his arm high, he motioned to two of his troopers to ease off to one side of the rattling, bouncing wagons. He led the other two mounted troopers off to the other side.

Together, seconds later, wagons and mounted cavalrymen smashed headlong into the dispersed tangle of confused Apaches.

Firing his Colt at paint-streaked savage faces inches away, driving steadily forward, McAllister registered only snatches of the next few hellish minutes. He slammed his mount against an Indian pony, bowling it over with its rider. He rode down another Apache who was on foot and trampled over him. He saw the lead army wagon drive a hole through Chata's milling, firing warriors and reach the rocks from which the guns of Ferguson and his hidden troopers spurted death at the Chiricahuas.

It had happened too fast, too unexpectedly, for Chata to collect his thoughts and his men. It was everyone for himself in that mad tangle of trampling mounts, screaming voices and roaring guns. McAllister's men had only one purpose: to get into the safety of those rocks up ahead. Chata's warriors had no such single purpose for the moment. Some turned to fight mounted troopers. Some fired at wagons. Some were racing off, intent still on getting away from the unexpected barrage from the rocks.

McAllister saw one of the big horses dragging Graff's freight wagon suddenly stop, then collapse on its belly. Graff snatched up his Spencer, shot a nearing warrior off his pony, then leaped away from the wagon and bounded into the canyon to the rocks, crouching low as he ran. The last army wagon skittered around the stopped freight wagon to get into the canyon mouth. From under the collapsed canvas on the freight wagon, Ellen Graff emerged, clutching her baby with both arms to her breast. She began to run clumsily towards the rocks. An Apache warrior kicked his pony toward her, raising his rifle like a club.

McAllister spurred over between Ellen and her pursuer. McAllister snapped up his Colt and fired, and saw the Apache's face well with blood as he fell backwards. Another warrior raced toward Ellen from the other side. Again McAllister swung in to serve as a shield, aiming the Colt and pulling the trigger. The Colt was empty. McAllister's horse slammed against the side of the Indian pony. He swung his Colt at the warrior's head. The Apache ducked, took the blow on his shoulder, his low-held rifle blasting. A tearing, burning shock went through McAllister's leg. He dropped the Colt and grabbed his saddlehorn with both hands to keep from falling as pain and weakness swept through him. He saw the Apache raise his rifle for a finishing shot. A small round hole suddenly appeared in the middle of the warrior's dark bare chest. He crumpled and thudded to the ground.

Holding on to the saddlehorn with all the ebbing strength left in his fingers and arms, McAllister kicked his mount towards the rock with his good leg. The other, his left one, dangled, streaming blood. Through blurred vision, he saw the driver of the last army wagon sprawl off, lifeless, to the ground. But the wagon was already up to the rocks. Someone leaped out and caught at the mules and forced them to keep pulling the wagon in through the rocks. It was Sergeant Ferguson.

A moment later, McAllister was urging his mount in through those blessed rocks. A trooper, seeing him sway in the saddle, grabbed the reins. McAllister got the toe of his good leg out of the stirrup, leaned against the saddlehorn and eased himself slowly down. He collapsed as soon as he touched the ground. Rockets of agony exploded through him. He stretched out on the hard earth and waited till his head cleared a little. Then he opened his eyes and saw the angle at which his wounded leg lay. It was broken.

Clenching his teeth, he sat up, leaning over to take the weight off his ruined leg. Then Sergeant Ferguson was kneeling beside him, ripping away the blood-soaked trouser leg, using it as a tournequet to stop the flow of blood. McAllister suddenly realized that the firing had ceased. Ellen Graff came over, crouching low, holding her crying baby.

"Can I help?" she asked with a voice like sandpaper.

"No, ma'am," Ferguson said. "I can handle this. You just take care of that baby."

"The water," she said. "My baby needs water."

Ferguson called to one of his troopers and told him to start taking survivors back to the water, one by one. "Start with Mrs. Graff."

As the trooper led Ellen back into the canyon, McAllister asked Ferguson, "How many men do we have left, Sergeant?" Ferguson had to lean close to make out the words through McAllister's clenched teeth.

"Seven, sir. And Graff makes eight."

"Oh, God!" McAllister moaned.

"Sorry, sir. I'm tryin' to straighten this bone a yours easy as I can."

McAllister leaned his head back against a rock, breathing hard. "Where's Chata?" He wished he could stand up to look over the rocks for himself. But he knew he wouldn't make it, not without passing out. It was all he could do to hold on to consciousness now.

Sergeant Ferguson told him, "They're all outside the canyon, just out of range. They're just waiting. Fifteen of 'em, I counted. We had 'em down to thirteen, but two more bucks showed up from the devil knows where. They got us bottled up in here for sure."

"For sure is right," McAllister agreed. "Could pick us off one by one if we tried to get out, outnumbering us like that."

"Never get the wagons out anyhow, sir. Them mules're dying. They'll never pull even a feather again. Sure hope Jess Remsberg gets the colonel back here in a hurry." Ferguson raised his head and yelled to a trooper: "Rip a stick of wood off one of those wagons for me to use as a splint."

"Jess got away all right, then?" McAllister asked.

Sergeant Ferguson nodded, but looked troubled. "Had three bucks on his trail, though. Last I seen, that horse of his was showing them how to run."

McAllister nodded. "I don't think there's any Indian pony that'll run that dun into the ground. Not with Jess riding him."

Millard Graff came back through the rocks and stood looking down at McAllister, his Spencer hanging down in his limp hand. His face was dark with fury.

"My wagon's out there. They'll probably set fire to it any minute."

McAllister looked up at him wearily, the flesh of his face sagging with pain. "Maybe not, Graff. They'll want whatever's in it first."

Graff sat down on the ground slowly, stared with sick fascination at what Sergeant Ferguson was doing to McAllister's leg. When he spoke again, his voice was surprisingly mild. "We're not going to get out of here, are we?"

"Maybe," McAllister told him, and then gasped as Ferguson suddenly straightened his leg. He waited till the surges of agony subsided, and murmured, "If we can hold them off a few days, we might get out. Some of us."

He shut his eyes against a wave of dizziness. His mind was dazed. His thoughts were with Jess Remsberg.

Jess reached the edge of the salt flat, drew up on the reins to give Lobo a breather. He narrowed his eyes to slits and stared across the wind-furrowed sands of the vast desert stretching ahead under an empty sky. It was a long way across; from where he looked, there seemed to be no end to it. It just kept going, clear to the bend of the horizon.

But it was the way he must go. It would take too long to try going around it. And he might not be able to, anyway. He turned in his saddle and looked back. There was dust rising over the crest of the long, low hill a mile behind him.

Those three Apaches weren't going to give up. They were ready to stick on his trail clear to Fort Duell, on the chance they might catch him before he reached it.

So far, Lobo had outrun their ponies. But there was a long way to go. Jess gave his attention again to the desert. A loathing for it filled him. Just looking at it made his throat burn, reminding him that he hadn't had a drink since leaving the canyon. He reached for his canteen. Just a little for himself, a little for his horse. It was going to take the rest of the day, pacing himself carefully, conserving the dun's strength through the blast of that desert heat, to get to the other side of it.

The light lift to the canteen told him what had happened, even before he saw the two small round holes drilled through its canvas cover.

One of their bullets had come too close.

Holding the empty canteen, Jess stared across the sands. That bullet, he thought, might just as well have struck his spine.

FOURTEEN

Death seizes a man with terrifying swiftness in the middle of the desert. Jess Remsberg's strength had been toughened and stocked with deep inner springs by long years of a hard life. But after two hours upon the sands, the pound of the blazing sun was already shriveling the core of his strength. He hadn't had a drop of water since just before sunup; it was now two hours past noon. His long legs hung leaden around the barrel of his coyote dun. His head was swelling against the constriction of his old Stetson.

The heat sucked sweat out of his pores before a drop of it moistened his skin. He was dry as the sand that was whipped against his lean, dark face by the wind. He narrowed his eyes against the cut of that flying dust, compressed his wide mouth to keep the grit from his swelling tongue.

When the dun stumbled under him again, Jess waited fatalistically. Lobo recovered, and trudged on. More slowly now. Each time more slowly. And there was no way the horse could be pushed harder than it could go.

Jess turned slowly in the saddle, kidneys aching with the movement. There was only sand as far as he could see. Not even a cactus relieved the threat of it. Hills of sand, valleys of sand, rivers of sand, shining white-hot under the driving glare of the yellow sun. A gigantic bake-oven with a yellowish bowl of sky for a clamped-down lid, to hold in the heat.

He squinted back for a long time before he saw the rising column of dust coming over the horizon back there. Dust that rose straight up before the wind caught it. It was different from the low clouds of swirling sand. This dust was stirred up by the hoofs of horses. They were unseen, but he knew there were three of them. Three ponies, three of Chata's warriors. They wouldn't quit following him. He couldn't lose them. They were following the tracks left by Lobo—tracks that led back across the sand as far as he could see, straight toward the rising column of dust. The dry, hot wind wasn't blotting out those tracks fast enough to cause his pursuers to lose the trail. Lobo was no longer leaving tracks clearly definable as hoofprints; now his tracks were merely long, deep furrows dragged through the sand. But those Apaches knew what they were—and would know why the tracks were changing. That knowledge would spur them on, if they'd been having thoughts before about turning back. They would know their quarry was slowing down.

There'd be no chance to shake them until night came. In the dark, he might be able to do it, if Lobo could last till dark. If he himself could last that long.

Without water? He looked up at the sun, flinched and quickly bowed his head, momentarily blinded. When his vision cleared, he brought himself around in the saddle and stared ahead, his narrowed eyes stinging. He squinted through shivering waves of heat at the distant blue hills edging the rim of the desert. They looked near enough to reach in a couple hours' riding. But Jess knew they were not. That was a desert illusion. Those hills were too far away to reach before dark.

His horse was exhausted, all energy sweated out of it. And he had no water. A sudden feeling of intense loneliness came over Jess. What the hell was he doing out here in the middle of this world of sand, moving across it to escape death, dying a little with each mile of it he crossed?

The dun faltered and stopped. For a moment, acceptance of death gripped Jess. Then a faint stab of fear went through him, followed by a weak rush of anger. He straightened and kneed Lobo into motion again. He pulled a tight rein on his nerves. If he let go, he'd be insane within the hour, and dead soon after that.

The pressing heat seemed to triple in weight with each minute. It bowed him over the saddlehorn gripped in his rope-scarred fingers. The skin of the backs of his lean hands was cracking with dryness. His throat seemed filled with grit. His tongue had become so swollen it felt as if it filled his mouth, pressing against his teeth.

Below him, Lobo's neck hung down till his muzzle trailed inches above the sand.

When darkness came, it brought such a flood of relief with it that Jess grinned. His lips split as they stretched over his teeth. Then he realized that it was dark only because his eyes were closed. He'd passed out. For how long? Seconds? Minutes?

He forced his eyes open. A flood of hot sunlight smote them a physical blow. Jagged pains drove back into his numbed brain. He clung to the saddlehorn while the sick churning of his stomach subsided.

The dun had stopped on top of a sand hummock.

Jess turned his head and looked back. For a moment, the distant hummocks heaved and swayed like ocean waves. Then they quieted and he could make out the rising column of dust thrown up by the Apache ponies. The dust was nearer now. But the Chiricahua warriors and their mounts were still hidden from his sight by the low-swirling, wind-pushed clouds of sand.

He kneed Lobo. The dun did not move. He tried a gentle slap against the dun's flank. The horse under him shuddered and began to sag.

Jess wrenched himself from the saddle. When he got the sand under his feet his knees trembled. His legs gave way under his weight. He sat down hard on top of the hummock. The dun stumbled down the sand slope and collapsed on his side, its legs and head stretching out stiffly. A stream of blood trickled from Lobo's open mouth and stained the sand.

Numbly, Jess watched the horse. Lobo had been his for over three years. A good horse. He looked back toward the nearing column of dust. Hate flooded him. He embraced it lovingly, rocking his shoulders slightly, letting it possess him, freshen him.

Jess knew he'd have to take on those three Apaches now. But it had to be under conditions of his own choosing, or he had no chance.

There was no involved planning, consciously, to what Jess did next. It came to him ready-made. He crawled down the side of the hummock to his dying horse.

Pulling his carbine out of the saddleboot, he staggered to his feet. His legs trembled, but they held him. He stared down at Lobo. The dun's bloodshot eyes were open, looking up at him pitifully. Jess wished he could give the horse the quick death of a bullet right away. But he couldn't risk it. There was no way of telling how far back the sound of a shot would carry across the desert floor.

Turning his back on the animal, Jess lurched up the sand slope. When he reached the top, he began plodding back the way he'd come, toward the oncoming Apaches.

Each step he took was a separate problem pierced through with the danger that his legs would give way under him. His strength was completely sapped. What was left was a dried-out shell, held together only by intense concentration. His progress was slow, but he placed his boots carefully, each time stepping into the dragging furrows left by Lobo's hoofs, dragging his own legs so the boots would not make distinct prints in the furrows.

There must be no sign to warn them that he was back-tracking. They would be able to detect it, of course, if they dismounted and squatted for a close look. He hoped they would see no reason to.

He went as far as his legs would carry him, to the bottom of a huge sand hummock. There he collapsed, his seared lungs wracked by dry panting that hurt his aching sides.

It took a few precious minutes to gather strength to drag himself up the slope of the hummock. Raising his head

cautiously over the top, he squinted through the shimmering
haze of heat and dust. Now he could see them—the shapes
of three ponies and riders, small in the distance, coming
toward him at a slow, steady clip.

An odd light flickered in Jess's eyes and became a steady
gleam. His lips thinned, and his face assumed a savage,
sullen intensity.

He knew they could not see the top of his head poking
above the hummock from that distance. But his horse
. . . Jess turned his head. The dun was hidden behind a
hill of sand.

Jess crawled halfway back down the slope and rested
there with his back against the sand. Leaning on one elbow,
he turned wearily on his side and began scooping a pocket
out of the slope. He pushed himself backward into this
hollow, burrowing deeper with the backs of his shoulders
and hips, till he was partially concealed.

In the hollow, in a half-sitting, half-reclining position, his
back was to the oncoming Apaches. He could see the
dragging tracks Lobo had made past the hummock to the
hill behind which he now lay. Unless they were looking for
it, he was sure they wouldn't notice that the hoof-furrows
had been disturbed by his backtracking to the hummock.

Jess levered a load into the carbine's chamber and placed
the carbine across his thighs. He drew the Colt from his
holster and drew back the hammer, cocking it. He pointed it
to the left, where the dragging tracks of Lobo led past his
place of concealment.

Then he waited.

It was an intolerably long wait. But he didn't become
nervous. His nerves were too limp for that. All of him that
could still function was concentrated on keeping his slitted,
burning eyes open. He was beginning to shiver with fever.

He heard them before he saw them—the steady, slow, soft
pad of hoofs in the sand. The gun was heavy in his hand. A
freak gust of wind tugged at the wide brim of his hat.
Otherwise, no part of him moved. He might have been part
of the sand.

They came past the side of the hummock riding side by side—dark, stocky young men on spotted ponies. Each wore knee-high moccasins and red headbands, like a rudimentary uniform, and each had drawn a big square of dirty cloth blanket shawl-like over bare shoulders, back and chest to keep off the sun. And each carried a rifle in his hand.

If one of them had glanced to their right, he'd have seen Jess quite plainly. But none of them did. They were all looking ahead, at the hill toward which the tracks led.

Jess felt no emotion but relief as he leveled the longbarreled Colt on the nearest warrior and squeezed the trigger. The revolver roared, the blast rocking against the barren sand. The nearest Apache bucked out of his saddle, his spine broken by the penetrating kick of the bullet. The other two turned instantly toward the shot, one of them yelling something as Jess thumbed back the hammer and fired again.

The warrior who had been riding in the middle screamed, reeling sideways in his saddle and clutching his stomach. His pony skittered away, whinnying with terror, and suddenly bolted into a wild run, throwing its rider off.

Jess snapped his Colt toward the third Apache, but the remaining warrior's pony was dancing sideways nervously, making its rider difficult to sight on. And the Apache, though taken by surprise, was already reacting with lightning speed. He was turned in his saddle, rifle up against his shoulder and firing, before Jess could get the sights on him.

The bullet slapped the hummock close to Jess's face, dashing sand against his cheek. Then Jess's Colt roared again, before the Apache could lever another load in. The Apache twisted in his saddle. A dark wet blotch spread over his chest, up near the shoulder. He fell sideways and hit the top of a sand hill on his back.

Jess started to recock his Colt. Suddenly, before he had the hammer back, the Apache moved, rifle still clutched in his hand, and rolled down behind the other side of the sand hill.

Jess snapped one shot at the hill with his Colt to keep the warrior down behind it. Then he reholstered his revolver and took up the carbine from his lap. The hillock behind which the Apache had hidden was a small one. A revolver bullet could not penetrate it from that distance. But a rifle bullet . . .

Jess aimed at the hillock. The carbine cracked three times before he heard a strangled cry from behind the hillock. Jess lowered the carbine. He was panting, and there was a dull pounding between his ears. Glancing away, he looked past the first Apache he'd shot, to the second one, who'd been thrown from his pony. He lay face-up, arms and legs sprawled, lifeless. Jess raised the carbine again, put another shot into the still form, for insurance.

Turning his head, he looked at the Apache ponies. One was far off, racing away across the desert. He looked at the other two ponies, moving about nervously nearby.

There was a dark horsehide water bag hanging from the saddle of the nearest one.

The presence of water gave Jess miraculous strength. He stood up with the carbine in his hands. His legs shook, but only a little; they'd carry him to that water. But first there was the Apache behind the sand hill to be sure of.

Jess plodded slowly past the body of the first Apache he'd shot. When he reached the hillock, he paused for only a second. He had to have that water. He took two swift strides around the hill, carbine ready.

The warrior was there. He'd been waiting for Jess. He sat on the ground with his back against the hillock, rifle in his hands, which lay on his lap. But he was past firing it. The sand absorbed his blood as it ran out of him. His head was tilted back and he stared up at the sun with wide-open eyes, not blinking.

Jess headed for the pony. It danced away from him, whickering nervously, eying him. Jess tried to speak soothingly, in Chiricahua Apache. What came out of his throat had the rasp of wood rubbing wood. But it must have meant something to the pony, for it quieted down and let Jess approach.

Jess had the water bag unstoppered in an instant. The water that filled his mouth was hot and tasted strongly of the animal skin that had held it, but it was the most delicious fluid he'd ever had.

He tried not to swallow any of it right off, but some of it trickled down his parched throat. He coughed, then strangled as the mouthful of water went down. The next moment he was on the ground, doubled over in an agony of dry retching.

The spasm passed, leaving him limp. He managed to sit up, holding the water bag between his dry hands. He held off as long as he could, then tried sipping more of the water. This time it went down better.

An hour passed, during which Jess did not try to rise from the sand. He sat there, slowly nursing himself with sips of water.

When he looked at the backs of his cracked hands and saw that they were beginning to sweat, he knew he was well enough to get moving. He stood up and capped the water bag, hung it back on the pony's saddle. There was enough left to last him.

The Apache pony held still long enough for him to mount up. He rode to the sand hill behind which Lobo lay. Around the dun's head the sand was damp with blood, but Lobo was still alive, breathing with broken harshness.

Jess dismounted. He took the long-barreled Colt from his holster and shot Lobo behind the ears, killing the horse instantly.

For a few moments he stared down at the dun, feeling empty and limp. Then he got on with it. It was a difficult job getting his saddle off the dead horse. He roped the saddle, with reins, bridle and saddlebags, behind the saddle of the pony. Remounting, he rode to the other Apache pony that had not run off, and roped it to the one he was riding. Then he rode away toward the blue hills that edged the other side of the desert. It was odd how much more real they looked, now.

FIFTEEN

The sun was getting low when Sergeant Ferguson scrambled back through the rocks to report what was happening. McAllister leaned back against a deep-shadowed rock, his splinted leg stretched out stiffly on the ground. The ruddiness was gone from his face, leaving only two fiery spots high on his cheekbones under his pain-narrowed eyes.

Ferguson squatted before him. There were deep lines of fatigue around his innocent, china-blue eyes, and his face had lost much of its plumpness.

"Lieutenant, some of 'em are moving up around the rim of the canyon back there."

"How many?" McAllister had to muster his strength to make his voice heard.

"Don't know, sir. All we've spotted is the dust of them moving around up there. But there's still plenty of 'em out on the flat, making sure we don't try getting out of here. Chata's with 'em out there. Spotted him through your field glasses. At least, I think it's him. Looks old as these rocks. Sure wish he was closer."

McAllister nodded, wishing he could climb higher among these rocks and have a look at the rim above for himself. "Sergeant, those bucks up top there may be planning to try getting down in here the way you did."

"They can try, sir," Ferguson said with satisfaction. "There's only one way down. It's slow, and they can't come that way more'n one at a time. Like we did. I got a man pegged down where he's got a clear, close shot at anybody tries to come down that way. Won't none of 'em make it. Hope they try.''

"They will probably wait for dark, Sergeant."

"Sure. Only there'll still be only one way down, one at a time. I already picked a couple of men to move back to the bottom there after dark. Any of those bucks come down're gonna back right into our boys and get themselves killed awful fast."

McAllister's bloodless lips fashioned a short smile. "Sergeant, I'll be recommending you for promotion to officer's rank when we get out of this."

Ferguson grinned. "Thank you, sir. I know you made it that way. Only right now all I'm lookin' forward to is being with my wife again, safe back in Duell."

"I know." McAllister himself had been thinking about the golden-haired girl he was to marry.

"Lieutenant," Ferguson said, "Mrs. Graff is asking for a gun. She says Chata's going to bury her alive if he gets hold of her again. She doesn't want to be taken alive."

McAllister gnawed at his lip and thought of Jess Remsberg. "All right, Sergeant. Give her a revolver. But tell her for God's sake not to use it till the last possible second. We've still got at least a fifty-fifty chance of lasting it out till the troops get here from Duell."

"I'll tell her that, sir. Tough on her . . . that baby and all. Her husband hasn't even . . ."

A rifle cracked, somewhere high above. The slap and whine of a bullet striking rock and bounding off close by followed while the shot still echoed through the canyon.

Ferguson threw himself face-down, then looked up foolishly. "I always duck when it's too late."

"Just remember to stay down from here on," McAllister rasped. "Sniping. That's what they're up there for. We can expect it from now on. Warn the others."

Ferguson rose to his knees, body bent, and bellowed: "Everybody keep down! They're starting to snipe at us! Stay in cover and don't move less you have to!"

Another shot sounded from up above. . . .

Back in the canyon, under a rock overhang near the pool of water, Ellen crouched, listening to the shots of the Apache snipers. They cracked singly, sparingly, with long intervals between. She was thankful that the shots did not waken her baby, asleep on the shaded grass beside her. Ellen knew that those snipers couldn't reach her under the overhang, yet each shot stabbed violently through her nerves. She wondered how long she could stand it without screaming.

The sniping had been going on for over an hour when she saw the dim figure of a man crawling toward her through the deep shade along the base of the canyon wall. It was not till he reached the overhang that she saw him clearly enough to recognize him as her husband.

Ellen stared at Millard Graff fixedly as he sat down just inside her shelter, a couple of feet away from her. He looked at her only long enough to meet her stare, then looked quickly away with color mounting on his cheekbones. She had never seen him look so unsure.

He took an Army Colt from his belt and held it out to her. "The sergeant told me to give you this," he mumbled.

She had to stretch her arm full-length to take the gun. She placed it on her lap and folded her hands over it.

Graff muttered, "I don't know why he told me to give it to you. He could've, himself."

"Perhaps he thought it was fit for you to," she said evenly. "You know what it's for."

He nodded. "I know. I think we're all going to die here."

He kept looking around him nervously, anywhere but at her or at the sleeping baby. It was obvious that he wanted to get away from his wife, but something held him for the moment.

At last he said, softly and without expression, "Ellen, I . . . I'm sorry everything turned out the way it did . . . for you and me."

"I am, too, Millard."

"I wish it could've been different. That I could have

taken it different than I did. I want you to know that, before . . . because we maybe won't be getting out of here."

"It couldn't have been different," she told him wearily. "I can see that now. Even now your feeling hasn't changed. Admit it. Even now you still can't help thinking I'd have done better to kill myself, than to come back to you from . . . from the bed of an Apache. Isn't that true?"

Graff stared down at his clenched hands, his face tight with unhappiness as his head jerked with a nod. "I know it's a rotten way to feel. But I can't help it."

"I know."

"Maybe if it hadn't been for that baby . . . you wanting to go get him. Maybe then we could've worked it out, in time."

Ellen shook her head. "You were a good husband to me, Millard, before the Chiricahuas took me. But you never would've been again. You never will be, no matter what."

Graff mumbled, "I've got to get back to those rocks now." He waited, expecting her to say something more. When she didn't, he began crawling away along the base of the canyon wall.

Ellen watched him go, fondling the metal of the gun on her lap. It was neither of their faults. It had just happened, and a wall had come between them that neither could ever have torn down.

Sergeant Ferguson crawled through the rocks to Lieutenant McAllister.

"We've spotted a couple of those snipers, Lieutenant. Wish we could locate the others. Must be at least four, five of 'em up there. But they keep shifting position."

A shot rang out, almost directly above their heads. The bullet spanged into the rocks a few feet away.

McAllister winced. "They're trying to work over to where they can fire directly into these rocks. If they can manage that, they'll be able to make us stay down when Chata's ready to charge us." He looked up at the darkening sky. "Be night soon, thank God."

Ferguson glowered at the sky. "Come dark, sir, we can set up a man on each side of the canyon here. Then when it gets light again, they can pick off any sniper that shows a head over the rim. Can't move 'em now. Them snipers'd have clear shots at 'em before they were set."

Another shot slapped down into the rocks near them. Rage suddenly, surprisingly, twisted all innocence out of Ferguson's face. Levering his carbine, he suddenly stood up—bringing the carbine against his shoulder, and turning toward the direction from which the shot had come—all in one swift, smooth motion.

The carbine cracked, bucking against his shoulder.

"Got him!"

"Get down!" McAllister barked. "Get the hell . . ."

Too late. McAllister saw the impact as the bullet punched into Ferguson's hat a split second before he heard the report of the rifle that fired it.

The carbine spilled out of Sergeant Ferguson's hands as he buckled to his knees, then flopped face-down, one arm falling against the sole of McAllister's boot. There was no need to turn Ferguson over for a look at his face, nor to remove his hat to see what the bullet had done to his head. It was final.

McAllister stared at his sergeant's body and found himself fighting an impulse to weep.

In the corner of the headquarters room at Fort Duell there was a tall, mahogany-veneer grandfather's clock, looking quite incongruous against the mud-plastered frame walls. Jess started hypnotically at its brass pendulum swinging lazily back and forth behind the glass panel. He sagged on the chair before the scarred wooden table, spearing forkfuls of hot beef and potatoes into his mouth from the steaming bowl of stew—and listened to the monotonous tick, tick, tick of the clock's pendulum. The hands of the clock pointed to nine minutes after eight. Through the room's single dusty window the full blast of morning sunlight flooded.

A little after eight in the morning. He had been riding steadily since sunup of the previous morning, except for the two hours he'd slept on the ground after reaching the hills on the other side of that desert. He hadn't wanted to spare himself those two hours, but he hadn't been able to stave it off.

The tall, thin corporal opened the door and came back in carrying a tray with a pot of coffee, and sugar and milk.

"Colonel said I should bring this," the corporal said. "He figured you needed it."

"I do." As the corporal left, Jess poured a cup of coffee, blended in a liberal helping of milk and two heaping spoonfuls of sugar. He drank it off in thirsty gulps, fixed himself another cup like it.

The door opened as Jess finished off the second cup. It was Colonel Foster, a compact officer in his early forties. He was quite bald, and his uniform looked as if it might have fitted him back when he weighed ten pounds more than he did now. The colonel opened a much-folded, worn map on the table.

"Show me," he snapped.

Jess leaned over the map for a moment, searching, then stabbed a fingertip to it. His hand showed the ingrained grime of the land he'd crossed. Colonel Foster rested his fists on the edge of the table and peered at the spot Jess was touching.

At last he said, "All right," and Jess removed his finger and poured another cup of coffee. This time when he drank it, it went down as though there weren't a stopper of solid dust blocking the way.

"Jess, can McAllister hold out till we reach him?"

"I don't know," Jess told him flatly.

Colonel Foster sighed and rolled up the map. "We'll be ready to move out in an hour. I know you're worn out, but you'll have to go with us."

"I want to."

"Corporal Thompson is bringing around a good, fast mount for you, Jess. But you can ride most of the way in one of the wagons, and get some sleep."

Colonel Foster started for the door. Jess said, "Colonel?"

"Yes?"

"You know the town marshal? Man named Clay Dean?"

"I know him. Very handy with a gun. Too damn handy. Why?"

"Private reason, Colonel. Is he in town now?"

"As far as I know. Killed a man last night, as a matter of fact. I'm sorry, Jess, but I must go now."

"Sure. Thanks." Jess watched the door close behind the colonel. He finished his third cup of coffee and stood up. The coffee was already beginning to perk him up. It wouldn't last long, he knew, against the weight of his exhaustion. But he didn't need long.

Automatically, his hand touched the hilt of his belt-sheathed knife. Then he drew the Colt from his holster, checked it, slipped it back. He limped to his carbine, leaning against the wall where he'd left it, but after a moment he decided against taking it along.

Outside, the whole post was in motion as cavalrymen got ready to move out under Colonel Foster. As Jess stepped off the boardwalk and started past suds row, Corporal Thompson hailed him. Turning, Jess saw the corporal leading a saddled horse across the parade ground through a confusion of sprinting cavalry troopers. Jess limped forward to meet him.

The horse was a clean-limbed, strong-looking sorrel mare. "Colonel says to present this horse to you with his compliments."

Jess patted the horse's head. The sorrel was well trained, did not shy away from the touch of the strange hand.

"Tell the colonel thanks." Jess swung himself up onto the saddle. "And tell him if I'm not here when he's ready to go, not to worry. If I'm a few minutes late, I'll catch up."

Jess turned the sorrel mare away through the parade ground without waiting for a reply, and headed off the post at a trot.

The town that called itself Duell, after the army post, was a couple of miles away—a sprawl of low frame and adobe buildings nestled between two bare hills. Jess found it hard to think about what he was going to do as he rode toward the town. Whatever he was going to do, he had only about an hour to do it in.

He took the sorrel to the top of the hill and pulled to a halt there, looking down at the town. Uncertainty flickered in him. An hour wasn't much time. Not enough time—if Clay Dean was the man who killed Singing Sky. Jess's fingers stroked the buckskin bag tied to his belt on his left hip.

Jess stared down at the town. He could wait till after he came back from the canyon with Colonel Foster. But he might not come back; he'd had more than his share of luck, lasting this long.

As his hand caressed the buckskin bag, the man who had murdered Singing Sky slowly became more real to him than McAllister, Ellen Graff, and the others far away in that canyon.

If he didn't get back here, the murderer would go unpunished. He'd live on, maybe remembering with pleasure what he had done to a helpless Indian girl.

Jess kneed the sorrel mare down the slope toward the town.

The town marshal's office was a frame room with a slanted roof, attached like an afterthought to the rear wall of the square adobe jailhouse. Finding the front door of the jail itself locked, Jess walked around the one-story building to the room at the rear. He tried its door and found it locked too.

His knock brought instant response from a sleep-fogged voice inside: "Who's that?"

"Jess Remsberg."

"Who the hell's that? And what d'ya want?"

"I'm riding scout for Colonel Foster at the fort," Jess shouted through the closed door. "Got to see you. It's important."

"All right." The man's voice was surly.

Jess waited. A full minute went by before the door opened. It opened wide, all at once, though Jess had not heard the drawing of the bar that locked it. The man who stood full in the open door facing him was big—taller than Jess and wider. His raw-boned face was wrinkled with sleep, and his long black hair was tousled and spiked. But he'd taken time to get on boots, pants and shirt, and to buckle a gunbelt around his wide hips. His gun wasn't in the holster, though. It was in his hand, aimed at Jess's stomach, the hammer cocked back.

Jess asked him, "Are you Clay Dean?"

"Yeah." Dean's eyes roamed Jess's face. Jess could see the marshal going back in his mind, making sure he didn't know Jess.

"What're you pointing that at me for?" Jess asked quietly.

"Just making sure," Dean said flatly. "There's plenty of men that'd like to . . . What're you waking me up this time of morning for?"

"I have to talk to you. Can I come in?"

Dean eased down the hammer and holstered his gun, but he kept his right hand as close as he could to it.

"I just got to sleep a couple of hours back," Dean growled. "Night's when I work, mostly. It better be important."

"It is."

Dean backed up, allowing Jess to enter. He closed the door behind him. One side of the room was taken up by a roll-top desk, a swivel chair with a torn leather back, and a standing gun-closet. On the other side was the bunk on which the marshal had been sleeping, and an old bureau with peeling paint. The back wall of the room was actually the rear wall of the adobe jail, with a door leading into the jail.

The marshal went over to the swivel chair and lowered himself into it, swinging about to face Jess. "Well? What is it? The colonel got a beef about my pistol-whipping his soldier boys when they acted up the other night?"

Jess studied the marshal briefly and pegged him for what he was: a killer, a ruthless gunfighter. That would be his sole qualification for the job he held. Jess had met the type before. In another part of this land, Clay Dean had probably been a criminal. He was one of those men who worked whichever side of the law seemed most profitable at the time.

"I need some information," Jess told him, moving close to the desk. "It's important to me."

"It better be important to *me*. Waking me up this early."

Jess held himself carefully, knowing the man before him was no less dangerous because he was sitting down. Clay Dean's right hand rested lightly on his thigh, inches from the butt of his holstered gun.

Keeping his face carefully expressionless, hooding his eyes so that Dean would see nothing in them to alarm him, Jess untied the buckskin bag from his belt.

"Chata's back across the border," he told the marshal. "Raiding again. Colonel Foster's getting ready to move out after him. He needs some information maybe you can supply." Jess opened the buckskin bag. The flesh of his hand crawled as he lifted out Singing Sky's hair. "The sutler says he bought this from you."

Dean glanced at the scalp, noting the white streak, the blue flannel in the thick braids, the tiny silver bells. His eyes darted back to Jess's face quickly. He looked puzzled.

"Yeah. He got it from me. Why?"

"Colonel Foster thinks it might help him to find out where you got it."

"Nothing I know can help him any. I won it in a poker game." Dean's eyes suddenly narrowed to slits, conjecture tightening his face as he stared at Jess. His right hand moved a bit closer to the butt of his gun. Some of the cold hate Jess had been trying to conceal had showed enough for Dean's hair-triggered instinct to sense it.

Jess felt a heaviness settling in him. He'd been so sure that Dean was the murderer; he looked the type. But he'd only won Singing Sky's hair in a poker game. Dean would have no reason to lie about it. There was no law in the land that would prosecute a white man for doing anything to an

Indian. And the way he'd said it, Jess was sure he was telling the truth.

Jess's throat felt suddenly tight and dry. "Who'd you win it from?"

Dean went on staring at him, suspicion and puzzlement plain on his face. "Why?"

"Colonel Foster wants to know."

"Don't sound right," Dean said. "Chata's Apache. That hair's from a Comanche gal. And it wasn't taken anywhere near here. Fellow I won it from told me."

"Who was it?"

Dean smiled thinly and said, "First tell me why. The truth."

Slowly, Jess replaced Singing Sky's hair in the buckskin bag and retied it to his belt, trying to find a lie that would relax the marshal's suspicions. But his nerves were too jangled for more trickery. His patience had worn too thin.

He looked at Dean again and said, "I want to know."

"Why?"

Jess grimaced with fury and blurted, "She was my wife!"

"Oh." The look of humor grew on Dean's face, striking Jess like a slap. "So that's it."

"Who was the man you got her scalp from, Marshal?"

"Friend of mine. I ain't about to tell you."

"I've got to know," Jess told him, his voice a choked whisper.

"Sure. So you can sneak up on him and kill him? I won't tell you. I'll tell *him*, though, when I see him."

Jess fought for control of himself. "I'll pay you for the information."

Dean shook his head. "You don't have that kind of money. The way I look at it, he did you a big favor. I got nothing against a man bedding with a pretty Indian girl. But when a man starts calling one of 'em his wife! Well, I don't think you're right in your head. He did you a favor, gettin' rid of her for you."

"Tell me his name!" Jess shouted, his control slipping badly.

The marshal's face tightened. "You can leave here now, friend. I'd get goin', if I was you."

Jess stared at him, unable to move.

"I said get out! And take that gun outa your holster and leave it here with me. I don't want you carrying a gun in my town."

Jess stood there, swaying slightly, saying nothing.

Dean's eyes probed at him. "You got five seconds to get shucked of that gun, friend."

Jess knew that Dean was deliberately giving him a chance to get his hand on his Colt, to try using it, the marshal was that sure of his own speed and deadliness. He'd welcome the excuse to kill Jess in self-defense.

Jess took the Colt from his holster, carefully, with the tops of his fingers. Holding it pointed away from Dean, he placed it on top of the desk. Dean grinned contemptuously and reached for Jess's Colt—reached for it with his right hand.

Jess kicked him in the face. His leg came jolting up, the heel of his boot slamming against the marshal's nose, mashing it in, the force of the kick driving Dean's head back, hurling him over to the floor with the swivel chair.

Jess fell to his knees, left hand grabbing the butt of Dean's holstered gun a split second before Dean's hand could close on it. In Jess's right hand was his knife, its point stabbing at the marshal's throat. Dean went down flat, the back of his head banging against the floor. The knife followed him down, stopped with its point touching the skin of his throat and staying there, drawing a tiny drop of blood.

Dean lay rigid on his back, staring up blankly into Jess's eyes. He held his arms stiff on the floor at his sides. His tongue crept out and licked his pale lips.

"Don't," the marshal whispered.

Jess drew Dean's gun from his holster. Kneeling with the knife pressed gently against Dean's throat, he said: "Tell me who you won her hair from."

"If I do?"

"If you do, you go on living, Marshal." Jess was breathing hard. His eyes were dull. "Maybe you're thinking you can just tell me any name that comes to your mind, then later come after me with a gun and shoot me down. That what you're thinking, Marshal?"

Dean stared up at him, saying nothing.

"You won't do that," Jess told him, hearing the way his voice trembled. "I can't let you do that. You got too much confidence in that gun-hand of yours."

Before Dean realized what was happening, Jess had dropped the gun and seized the trigger finger of Dean's right hand, bending it back, not giving him time to brace against it.

"No! Wait!"

Jess's shoulder rose an inch, driving pressure down his arm to the hand bending back Dean's finger. The bone went with a dry snap.

Dean screamed. His body bucked, fell back instantly as the motionless knife dug into his throat, drawing a thin stream of blood. Dean lay there under the knife, rigid, eyes squeezed shut against the pain running up his arm from his dangling finger, moaning thinly through clenched teeth.

"Now you know," Jess whispered, his face a mask of malicious hate. "You're not fast any more, with that hand ruined. You won't come after me. I'll come after *you*—if you give me a wrong name. Lie to me, and I'll come back and cut your face to ribbons with this knife."

Dean's eyes opened wide, suddenly filled with fear, like a lion with its fangs and claws drawn. "I don't owe him a thing! Why should I cover for him? You didn't have to . . ."

"Who is he?"

"A freighter. Name's Graff. Millard Graff."

Jess stared down at him, his brain rocking with the shock of it. He pressed the point of the knife a bit more firmly against the bleeding throat.

"You're lying!"

"I'm not! Why should I . . ."

"I think you're lying to me."

"No! Look, ask Ernie Unger. He was in the game. Graff ran outa money. He needed two more dollars to see my hand. He put up the scalp for it. Ask Ernie!"

"Where do I find Ernie?"

"Blacksmith shed. He's our blacksmith."

Jess got his free hand on Dean's gun and stood up. The shock was still washing through him. Holstering his own Colt, he looked down at Dean, who sat on the floor cradling his broken hand against his chest.

"Don't come after me," Jess told him. "I see you again, I'll kill you. If you lied to me, you won't have to come after me. I'll find you."

He opened the door and went outside, heading around the side of the jail to the town's main dirt street. He dropped Dean's gun by the side of the jail.

The blacksmith's shed was at the other end of the town, near the town corral. Jess heard the clang of hammer on anvil as he limped toward the big opening in the frame wall that served as a doorway for horses and men. Inside, he found a man at work beside the fire, reshaping an iron wagon tire.

The blacksmith was stripped to the waist, torso and arms shiny with sweat. He was fat and powerful, with a slack, fleshy face. When Jess came in, the blacksmith put down his hammer and tongs, wiped his hands on his dirty apron and smiled cheerfully.

"What can I do for you?"

"The marshal sent me over to check on something. You're Ernie, ain't you?"

"Yeah."

"Remember being in a poker game with the marshal, when he won an Indian girl's scalp?"

"Sure. Couple months back that was. Maybe longer. I don't remember exactly."

"Who'd the marshal win that scalp off of?"

Ernie's fleshy face creased with uncertainty. "Why would

the marshal send you over here to ask me? He could've told you himself."

Jess took the Colt from his holster, cocked it, and aimed it at the blacksmith's thick middle. "I got no time to waste," he snapped, voice crackling with an irritation that was close to hysteria. "Who'd he win that scalp from?"

Ernie's eyes went wide. He went back a step, staring at the pointed gun as though hypnotized by it. "It was Millard Graff," he blurted.

"You sure?"

The blacksmith nodded, not taking his eyes from the gun aimed at him. "Sure. Graff was drunk, showing it off. Said he took it off a Comanche girl he caught alone and . . ."

Jess turned away and limped quickly out of the shed, into the broiling heat of the sun. Tiny bubbles of pain were exploding behind his eyes.

SIXTEEN

Pushing the strapping sorrel mare along fast, Jess caught up with Colonel Foster's company of cavalry eleven miles out of Fort Duell. He passed two mule-drawn army wagons on the way; the colonel didn't want to slow himself up with them, so they were following behind, making pretty good time since both wagons were empty. They were for bringing back wounded, and the ammunition, in case both still existed and McAllister's wagons were wrecked.

When Jess caught up with the cavalry company, he found that Colonel Foster was really stripped for speed. Each trooper had two horses. One wagon, carrying food and water, was with them—pulled along at a good clip by six hulking Conestoga horses.

Colonel Foster, leading the way on a tall bay, glanced at Jess as he drew up beside him. "What happened to you, Jess?" The colonel looked angry.

"Sorry," Jess told him. "Couldn't help it."

"Personal affairs have to wait at a time like this."

"This couldn't wait."

Colonel Foster's mouth drew thin. But after a moment he said, "You look like hell, Jess. Why don't you crawl into the wagon and get some sleep? The wagon'll stay with us till tonight. Then we'll pick up the pace and run on ahead of it."

"Not sleepy, sir. But thanks."

Colonel Foster shrugged and gave his attention to the

terrain ahead. Jess drew off a bit to be by himself, keeping the sorrel at a run to stay with mounts of the troopers.

Jess rode with conflicting emotions storming inside him. Both Ellen and Millard Graff were in that canyon. And he prayed for both to be still alive and unhurt when he got there.

His desire to see Millard Graff dead amounted to a savage lust. But he had to see Graff die; die by his hand. He would have to die very slowly to satisfy the grief and fury in Jess.

But something else tore at Jess—the fear that Ellen might be dead. And he couldn't straighten out which was stronger in him, his fear or his hatred.

He had been riding hard for over an hour with those twisted, tormenting passions jangling inside him, when exhaustion finally broke through and engulfed him. When he realized that he was swaying dangerously in the saddle, his vision blurring, he dropped back to the rattling supply wagon.

Hitching the sorrel to the tailgate with a long lead rope, Jess switched from the saddle to the wagon, crawling in under the high-hooped canvas. There, on the hard, jolting boards of the wagon bed, he sank into the oblivion of a fatigue-drugged sleep.

It was the halting of the wagon that finally awakened him. Looking out over the tailgate, Jess saw that it was night. His whole body was stiff and sore, and his joints felt as if they were breaking when he moved them to climb out of the wagon. But with movement stirring his blood, the use of his own limbs came back to him steadily. He limped over to where the troopers were gathered, and joined them in a quick, cold meal.

Colonel Foster made sure each man refilled his canteen to the brim from the water casks in the wagon. Assigning one of his troopers to ride with the driver of the wagon team, the colonel turned the extra mount over to Jess.

"From here on," the colonel said, so all could hear him, "we *ride*."

They did. The jolting wagon was left far behind within

the hour. It was still dark when they reached the edge of the desert. Stopping there only long enough to transfer themselves and their riding gear to their spare mounts, they set out fast across the desert. Colonel Foster wanted to cross as much of it as possible before the sun rose to slow them up.

Jess led the way. He knew they were making much better time than he had alone, coming from the other direction. But they still had a long way to go.

The sun was nearing the top of its burning rise across the sky. Its blazing brilliance beat straight down into the canyon, upon the backs of the pitiful handful of men stretched out on the ground with their rifles pointed out through the rocks, waiting. Further back in the canyon, near the seep-fed pool where the two wagons stood, the sun poured down past the shelter under which a woman sat, tense and still, clutching a baby and an army revolver.

Millard Graff, stretched out close to Lieutenant McAllister, stared bitterly out across the heat-baked flat.

"McAllister," he said, "maybe they've gone away."

"No they haven't." McAllister's leg throbbed with steady pulses of numbing agony. The bandage binding its splint was bright with blood. The wound had opened wide when he'd moved it to help beat off Chata's attack the previous evening.

Chata had depended upon his snipers to keep McAllister busy during that attack. But McAllister had finally managed to place a man at the base of each wall siding the canyon entrance. From there, each had had a clear view of the opposite rim. When the snipers showed themselves to fire down into the rocks, the two troopers had begun picking them off.

That had ended effective sniping. The surviving Apache marksmen had been forced to withdraw from the rim, to positions from which they could not sight straight down at the men bedded among the rocks.

The attack had cost Chata at least six warriors, but it had left McAllister with only four troopers, plus Graff and his wife. Not enough to stand off another attack, if Chata pressed it home reckless of cost. Entrenched as they were, McAllister knew, they would take a disproportionate toll before they died.

Whenever he shut his eyes now, McAllister saw the faces of those who were already dead. Dead because of him. Their deaths meaningless—unless Colonel Foster arrived soon enough to catch Chata here. McAllister did not shut his eyes often, now.

Graff suddenly said, "I don't see them anywhere out there."

"They're there," McAllister sighed. "Depend on it."

Graff turned on him angrily. "They *could* have just decided they've cut us down enough, and headed back north. Couldn't they?"

"Not Chata," McAllister told him. "He wants the ammunition in our wagons. And he wants to finish us, to the last man. Maybe that even more than the ammunition. With all the men he's lost, he's got to finish us all the way to claim a victory. And if he can't claim a victory when he has us outnumbered, he won't be such an important chief any more. The bucks'll stop running to join up with him."

Graff spat dryly and glared back across the flat. "Well, if he's out there, why doesn't he hit us? What's he waiting for?"

"Who knows? Maybe for the same reason he can't quit now. Lost too many men. Chata's most likely having a tough time bracing his warriors for another charge. They know what it'll cost 'em to take us. They didn't join Chata to get themselves slaughtered. They thought they were going to do the slaughtering."

"I wish to hell . . ." Graff said in a loud voice, suddenly choked off. When he spoke again, quickly, it was a whisper: "Here they come!"

McAllister had heard for himself. The sudden pounding of ponies' hoofs. The next instant he saw Chata and his warriors come racing around the curve of a nearby hill, charging head-on at the mouth of the canyon. They grew bigger every second. Awfully big. There weren't so many of them now, but there were plenty for what Chata wanted to do.

McAllister shouted no orders. There was no need. Each man could be counted on to fight for his own life, to lie there in the rocks and fire as fast and straight as was humanly possible. And that was all there was left for them to do.

Touching his finger lightly against the trigger of his carbine, McAllister watched the rapidly nearing Apaches, gauging the distance, waiting for them to get within range. They came crouched low, headbands barely visible above the outstretched necks of their ponies. McAllister knew he'd better wait till they were quite close. The agony throbbing up from his leg was making him too shaky for accurate shooting at anything but short range. He leaned his cheek hard against the carbine stock, watching them over his sights.

Suddenly, as a trooper in the rocks tried the first tenative shot, Chata and his warriors wheeled at an angle and raced off to the left. Moments later they had vanished from the flat—that part of it that could be seen from inside the canyon.

Graff glanced at McAllister. "What're they . . ."

"How the hell do I know!" McAllister growled.

Minutes crawled by with no further sign of Chata. McAllister lay still, feeling the thud of his heart against the ground. His hands became slippery on the carbine. The Chiricahuas stayed out of sight, off against the wall of the mesa somewhere.

McAllister felt another wave of dizziness moving through his brain, and set himself to fight against going under. He began to curse quietly, through clenched teeth.

He stopped cursing abruptly, and the dizziness vanished. The rear of a wagon was moving slowly into sight at the left wall of the canyon mouth.

"My wagon!" Graff rasped. "They're pushing it in . . ."

But McAllister was already yelling for the others in the

rocks to hear: "Aim at the wagon! They're using it for cover!"

The crash of seven rifles from the rocks sounded almost as one heavy shot. Graff's wagon kept moving, more of it coming into view.

Despair possessed McAllister. Chata had found a way to charge without losing most of his men before they reached the rock barricades.

Graff's wagon had been sitting out there all this time. After one of the two horses pulling it had been downed, the other had kept moving, wild with fright. Before the second horse had been killed, it had dragged the wagon and its dead teammate off to the left, out of the view of the men among the rocks. The Chiricahuas hadn't fired it. Chata wanted the goods in it, figuring on taking it when the fight was won.

But now Chata had found a better use for Graff's wagon.

Cutting the dead horses away from the traces, Apache riders had tied their ponies to the wagon tongue, facing backwards. Now those riders were kicking their ponies forward, pushing the wagon—rear end first—into the canyon. And, McAllister was certain, there'd be more of Chata's warriors inside the wagon, buried among Graff's goods for protection.

The wagon would be driven against the rocks. The warriors in the wagon could then leap out, right in among McAllister's men, keeping them busy while the rest of the Apaches charged into the canyon with the heavy bulk of the wagon giving them fairly good protection.

"Fire for those ponies!" McAllister shouted as the wagon turned full into the canyon and began to move backward toward the rocks. "Get their legs!"

He was firing himself as he yelled, aiming low under the wagon bed. But he knew how hopeless it was. The ponies' legs—that was all that could be seen of them, moving legs at that, obscured by the dust they kicked up. But the crashing of shots around him told him the others were trying their best.

The wagon was gaining momentum as it rattled nearer to

the rocks. Five rifle barrels came poking out from under the
canvas, firing at McAllister's tiny defending force. It must
have been a signal. Around the corner at the canyon mouth
came Chata and a cluster of mounted warriors, howling and
firing their rifles as they wheeled in after the wagon.

It was then—through the yelling and the firing that
bounced back and forth off the narrow rock walls—that the
most beautiful sound he'd ever heard reached his ears—a
cavalry trumpet, sounding the charge.

Chata and his warriors heard it too. Charging ponies
bucked to a stop. Graff's wagon halted. For a second, all
firing ceased, on both sides. The next second, the canyon
mouth became a cauldron of confusion as ponies wheeled
and tangled, Apaches appeared from under the wagon's
canvas and leaped to the ground—all fighting to get out of
the canyon mouth at the same time—while the seven men
bedded among the rocks poured a murderous, joyous fire
into their backs.

Seconds later, Colonel Foster's cavalrymen bowled into
the Apaches as they scrambled out of the canyon and
scattered for escape on the open flat.

Jess, racing in with the first of the mounted troopers, bore
the first shock of the clash as cavalry and Apaches slammed
into each other. Using his Colt alternately as a firearm and a
club, Jess found himself caught in a wild tangle of colliding
Indian ponies and army horses, of roaring guns and troopers
and Apaches grappling hand to hand. He shoved, trampled
and blasted a path through the surging mass, fighting into
the canyon, toward Ellen, ears stuffed with the clamor, eyes
burned by gunsmoke and the swirling dust kicked up by
frantic hoofs and dragged bodies.

The barricade rocks were in sight ahead of him when a
pony rammed into his sorrel mare. Jess ducked instinctively, twisting in the saddle. A slashing rifle butt clubbed his
hat from his head. Jess swung the heavy Colt in his hand,
saw an Apache face jerking back, away from it. He stopped
the swing in mid-air, squeezed the trigger with the Apache
face inches from the Colt's muzzle.

He didn't see what the bullet did to the warrior's face. He felt something strike the back of his head, and saw only pitch-black darkness in front of him. He felt consciousness retreating as he fell from the saddle. He didn't feel his face slam against the ground.

SEVENTEEN

The first time Jess opened his eyes, he was aware only of Ellen's vague face above him, of her eyes looking down at him. He was not even aware that he had reached for her till he felt his hand tightening around hers.

"The boy?" he whispered.

She smiled. "He's all right. With one of the officers' wives. I'd forgotten there were people so ready to help when . . ."

But Jess had already slipped back into dark oblivion.

When he awoke the second time, she was still there.

This time he said, "Your husband?"

"He's alive. Not hurt." Jess couldn't make out her expression when she said that.

"That's good," he whispered, and the undertones in his voice made her look at him sharply, not understanding. She saw nothing in his face. His eyes had already closed again. His mouth, tightened for a fraction of a second, relaxed instantly into the softness of a deep sleep.

An army surgeon was changing the bandage on the back of Jess's head when he came fully awake again. This awakening was different from the others. He lay on his stomach, and the creased, sweat-stained sheet of the narrow bunk under him came sharply to his sight. His mind was as clear as his vision.

He started to turn his head.

"Stay still!" the doctor snapped.

Jess folded his forearms under his chin and felt the quick fingers of the doctor pressing the bandage securely against a soreness at the back of his scalp.

"What happened to me?" Jess's voice was weak.

"Bullet creased your thick skull. It's a fairly deep wound. It gouged the bone, but didn't break it. The wound itself hasn't done you much harm."

"I sure been out cold a long time, for it not to be doing me much harm."

"That was the impact of the bullet against your skull. You've had a bad concussion. You'll be all right. You can turn over now."

Jess rolled over on his back. His muscles felt like water, but there was no pain. Even the back of his head felt no worse than if he'd bruised it in a light fall.

He saw now that he was in a small, stuffy room with mud-plastered walls and a single small window through which hot sunlight poured. Turning his head, he saw his clothes, saddlebags and gunbelt hanging from wall pegs. His carbine stood in a corner.

As the surgeon pulled the sheet up to his chest, Jess said, "This Fort Duell?"

"That's right. This is Lieutenant Murray's quarters. He's sharing other quarters so you can have some quiet."

"I feel pretty good now."

"You should. You've had two days rest."

"My God! . . . What happened to Lieutenant McAllister?"

"He's here. Right next door to you."

"He okay?"

"No. Broken leg. Try sitting up."

Jess got his elbows under him and shoved himself up, leaning back against the headboard.

The doctor asked, "Feel dizzy?"

"No. I feel fine. Can I go see McAllister?"

"Later. Just try sitting up for a while. If you take things by easy stages, you'll be as good as new in a few days."

The growling of Jess's stomach was heard plainly by both of them. They grinned at each other.

"I'm empty," Jess said.

"Should be. She's been spoon-feeding you whenever you came half awake, but she didn't get much into you that way."

"She?"

"Mrs. Graff."

Jess looked at the closed door, remembering. "Where is she?"

"Getting some sleep, most likely. I shooed her out of here when I came in. She'd been here most of the time you have. I found her asleep in that chair."

While Jess thought about that, the doctor closed his bag and stood up. "I'll have a good meal sent up to you in a few minutes. Shall I give your regards to Lieutenant McAllister? I'm tending to him next."

"Yeah. Thanks."

After the doctor left, Jess sat there on the bed just staring at the sun-filled window, thinking of Ellen Graff. And Millard Graff. He had no feeling of urgency about Graff. The freighter was alive and in Fort Duell. Jess felt he wanted to wait now, till his strength came back. Then he'd be ready for Graff.

A trooper brought him his meal on a tray, left it with him. Jess wolfed it down. Then, feeling pleasantly full and relaxed, he took his time with a second cup of coffee. Shoving the tray to the foot of his bunk, he swung his legs over the side and tried standing up. It wasn't bad, though his legs were weak.

He walked slowly over to the wall pegs, got his clothes, and carried them back to the bunk. Sitting on the edge, he got into his pants and shirt. He looked for a moment at his boots, decided it was too much trouble. Barefoot, he padded slowly out of the room, down the covered board-walk outside to the next door. He opened it and went inside.

It was a room exactly like his own. McAllister sat on the bunk, propped back against two pillows, legs stretched out straight on top of the sheets. One leg was completely confined in a huge cast.

"Hi!" Jess said, closing the door and grinning. "How's the general?"

McAllister grinned back. "Hi, yourself. You ain't supposed to be out of bed yet."

"My legs feel as if I just been born." Jess sat himself on the edge of McAllister's bunk. "How's it feel, Gil?"

"Hurts like hell. How's your head?"

"A hangover feels worse. But I missed most of the fun. The colonel clean up Chata's band?"

McAllister nodded. "Chata got away, though. Most likely with a couple of his bucks. Not many, that's sure."

"Too bad he slipped out of our fingers," Jess said. "He's probably back in Mexico by now, licking his wounds."

"I don't think we'll have to worry about Chata any more," McAllister told him. "After the beating he got, his reputation with the Apaches is going to be mighty small. He'll never be a big chief again. Just an old man."

Jess patted the cast on McAllister's leg. "Guess that's worth this, Gil. You did what you set out to do. Pinned Chata down long enough for Colonel Foster to show up and finish him. How's it feel to be a hero?"

McAllister's face clouded. He looked away from Jess, at the wall. He said softly, "It doesn't feel so good, Jess."

Jess stared at him. After a moment he said gently, "I'm sorry about that, Gil."

McAllister turned his head and met Jess's eye. "I killed most of my men."

"You're mixed up, Gil. Chata killed them."

"I took 'em into it. I got them killed to feed my army career."

"You're an officer, damn it!" Jess snapped. "You know how many families Chata would have wiped out, slaughtered, tortured, if you hadn't stopped him where you did! You did what the army's out here to do—make this land safe. You did your duty. And a damn good job, too."

"I know," McAllister admitted. "But it's a terrible

responsibility, Jess. A man that's not an officer doesn't realize. I didn't, before. All I was responsible for, before, was my own skin."

"You wanted to be an officer. I guess that's what it's got to cost you."

McAllister nodded and looked away again. Jess, seeing that he wanted to be alone for a while, stood up.

"I'd better get back to my bunk, Gil."

"Sure. See you later. When they let me up on crutches, we'll go into town and get drunk together."

"Good idea. It'll be on Sergeant Ferguson. He promised to buy the drinks for me if I got the colonel back on time."

McAllister looked at Jess bleakly. "It wasn't on time for Ferguson, Jess."

Jess's eyes narrowed. He left without speaking.

The sunlight at his window was beginning to fade when Ellen opened the door and entered his room. She was startled to see Jess stretched out on the bed with his pants and shirt on.

"Jess! Have you been out of bed?"

He sat up quickly, smiling at her. "Just trying out my legs."

"Doctor Raphael says you're to stay in bed at least till tomorrow."

"Nothing wrong with my legs that moving around won't cure."

She started for the chair. He patted the mattress beside him. "Sit here, Ellen."

She looked at him for a moment, then sat on the edge of the bunk.

"Thanks for nursing me. How's the baby?"

"I just fed him. He's playing with Mrs. Olaf's children. She's the one who lent me a crib for him."

"I told you it's a big country. Remember? It ain't so hard to go someplace where people're ready to treat you decent."

"They'll know about me here, soon. I wonder how they'll act then."

The sudden edge of bitterness in her voice stabbed at his heart. "There're places further away, Ellen. I guess we've got a lot to talk over."

She bit her lip, looking away from his probing eyes. "Yes," she said softly. "But that can wait for a while."

"Some things can't wait," he told her. He felt the fear building up in him, the desire to postpone it. But it was something that had to be faced. "How's your husband feel about you spending all your time with me the past couple days."

"He didn't know." She still wouldn't look at him. "He was busy. Colonel Foster lent him a couple of army horses to haul his wagon here. He didn't come near me after we got here. He slept in the wagon." Suddenly, Ellen met Jess's eyes. "And now he's gone."

"Gone!" Jess sat up straighter, rigid.

"He sold everything in his wagon to the sutler here. Bought some mules for his wagon and headed back to Avalanche. The colonel says the way's pretty safe now, with Chata's band destroyed. Millard left a few hours ago. I just found out."

Jess stared at her for a few moments, feeling it build up inside him. "He didn't take you with him."

"No," Ellen said quietly, her face expressionless. "He didn't ask me to go with him."

"Suppose he had asked you?"

"I don't know. I wouldn't have wanted to go with him."

Jess looked down at his lean hands. They were clenched into tight fists. He opened his fingers with an effort, glanced at his gunbelt hanging from the wall peg, then at his carbine standing in the corner.

"I'll have to go after him," he said.

She was puzzled. "Why?"

Jess looked at her, wished fervently that he could keep it from her. That he could just do it, and never let her know. But he couldn't do it that way. Not with what he felt for her, the way things were between them. He couldn't spend the rest of his life hiding a secret that big from her. She had to know, and decide what to do knowing it.

"I found out who killed Singing Sky," he told her softly. "Murdered her. Raped her. Scalped her. Your husband. He did it."

He watched the shock of it hit her.

"Millard?" Her voice crawled with horror. "Millard did . . . No! You're wrong!"

Jess shook his head. "I found out. Two different men told me. He lost her hair playing poker. Boasted about how he got it. He was drunk, and he told them about it."

"Oh, God in heaven!" She shuddered as though a chill had gone through her. Her face was twisted into a grimace.

"So you see what I've got to do, Ellen. I've got to kill him."

"Jess. No! You can't. I . . ." She gasped for breath, fought to control herself. When she spoke again at last, her voice was quieter, held in tight restraint. "Please, Jess. You mustn't."

His face became a sullen mask. "I'm going to. Nothing can stop me."

"I'm begging you, Jess. Don't. We both know what we feel for each other. It couldn't still be that way if you . . ."

"That's too bad," Jess told her, bitingly. "But that won't stop me. I hope you can get over feeling that way. But whether you do or you don't, I'm gonna kill him."

"That won't accomplish anything," she pleaded. "All you'll do is make yourself like he is. He did . . . what he did, because the Apaches captured me. He did it for revenge. Now you want to kill him for revenge. Is that any different?"

"You know it is," he said impatiently.

"Jess, you once told me I had to forget the past, find a new life for myself. Now I'm telling you the same thing."

Jess looked down at his hands, fought to calm the raging inside him, the cursing at fate. Talking wouldn't do any good. It was leading them nowhere.

Ellen whispered. "Jess? Will you do it? Will you hold back for me?"

Jess leaned back against the pillow, stared up at the ceiling.

"Jess?"

He made his voice lazy: "I don't know. I'm tired. Guess all the walking around wore me out. Afraid I'm gonna fall asleep on you."

"All right, Jess." She said it uncertainly, not knowing whether she had persuaded him or not.

She watched him close his eyes. In a few minutes, his face relaxed. His chest rose and fell with his heavy, steady breathing. She got up quietly and stood looking down at him.

She left the room and walked slowly to Mrs. Olaf's quarters, lost in thought. She kept turning it over in her mind, searching for words that would sway Jess, as she fed her baby and put him to sleep in the crib, as she ate her own supper with Mrs. Olaf.

When she'd finished the dishes, Ellen could hold back no longer. She went quickly to Jess's room.

Jess was gone. Her heart was thudding sickeningly as she looked at the wall. His gunbelt, saddlebags and carbine were gone, too.

Ellen rushed out of the room and hurried to tell McAllister what had happened.

EIGHTEEN

He rode hard through the night, the pounding of the sorrel's hoofs driving upward through his body and stabbing into his fevered brain. And as he rode, his purpose grew till it filled him completely.

The darkness was little hindrance to him. He knew the trail Millard Graff was traveling, and he knew Graff would be slowed by his wagon. He'd catch Graff before he reached Avalanche.

It seemed to him that this was the way it must be, not in Fort Duell, or in Avalanche, but out here somewhere, between the two of them. Just the two of them, alone in this savage, empty land of stone and sand.

The pain of his head wound increased with every mile. But so did the fire in his brain, fed by vivid, hate-filled images of Graff killing Singing Sky. After several hours it was this hate alone that kept him in the saddle.

When, finally, he passed out for a moment, coming to just in time to stop himself from falling, he knew he must stop and rest. Stretching out on the hard ground, he fell asleep instantly. But it was a sleep torn by nightmares so violent that they awakened him after little more than an hour.

Climbing back onto his saddle, Jess rode on through the darkness. Millard Graff, somewhere up ahead of him, pulled him on like a magnet. At dawn, he found Millard Graff's wagon.

It lay on its side in a shallow arroyo between two gaunt white-sandstone buttresses. The mules were dead in the traces, their blood drained out through the long knife-slashes that had opened their throats.

Millard Graff was not there. Jess rode a slow circle around the sandstone cliffs without spotting any sign of him. Returning to the wagon, he lowered himself to the ground and began studying the tracks there. He sorted them out, and read from them what had happened.

The wagon had swung in here, going fast. Too fast. The wheels on one side had sunk into the soft bottom of the arroyo, overturning the wagon. The tracks of four Indian ponies led into the arroyo, coming from the same direction as the wagon. Where the tracks of the ponies led out of the arroyo, one was carrying a good deal more weight than the other three. They had taken Graff with them.

Jess dragged himself back up onto the sorrel, and began following the pony tracks. He knew he wouldn't have to follow for long. They wouldn't take Graff far.

The tracks led him through stands of solitary buttes fronting a connected range of low red-and-gray mountains. An hour later he was following them through a dry, rock-strewn creek bed that twisted its way between towering, roughhewn cliffs that shut out most of the sunlight. He had been moving along this creek for an hour when he heard an agony-distorted scream.

The hairs at the back of Jess's neck stood up as a chill traced its icy fingertip along his spine. He jerked the sorrel to an abrupt stop. The scream sounded again, lasting longer than seemed humanly possible.

Jess dismounted quickly, tethered the sorrel, and drew his carbine from its boot. He moved ahead on foot, toward the scream. After almost five minutes' walking, he turned a corner in the canyon and found the way ahead almost blocked by piles of mammoth boulders, the way through them barely wide enough to let a horse through. He was going toward the opening when the scream came again. Close. Jess stopped, hesitated, then turned and made his way towards one wall of the canyon.

At the base of the cliff, he began climbing the boulders.
The screams began to come more closely together, till they
beat against each other almost continuously. And yet did not
diminish in their piercing intensity. He had to hang onto his
nerves to keep climbing.

When he reached the place where the boulders leveled
off, Jess stretched out on his stomach, clutching the carbine
tight in one hand. He began inching himself forward with
his elbows and legs. At the edge, he found himself looking
down into a shadow-darkened chasm among the boulders.

A small fire burned on the floor of the canyon down
there. Its light flickered against tethered ponies. And close
by the fire, it glowed fiercely against the faces of four
crouched Apaches. Jess could see them clearly. They were
near enough for him to see exactly what they were doing to
the naked man staked down beside the fire. One of them
was Chata.

Jess knew then that he and the army had been wrong.
Instead of heading south for Mexico, Chata had played it
smart and ridden north, where the army wouldn't be looking
for him. Millard Graff, going north also, had run into Chata
and his four remainng warriors. And to them, Graff was
something on which they could vent the pent-up rage that
they felt at their defeat.

For it was Millard Graff they had staked down beside the
fire, howling like some inhuman being in the pit of hell
under their heated knives.

Jess watched. Cold perspiration beaded his forehead and
ran in rivulets down his face. This was the horror he had
planned for Graff. Except that it was Chata and the last of
his band doing it, instead of himself. He had only imagined
it: this was what it was like in reality. His hands were
becoming slippery with sweating.

This was what Jess wanted for the man who had killed
Singing Sky—a slow, agony-filled death. Yet as he
watched, his mind began to blank, refusing to accept and
register what he saw.

Graff was dying now. No matter what happened, he could
not go on living after what had already been done to him.

But the Apache methods would hold off his death for a long time.

Jess tried to keep thinking of Singing Sky. He fought to remember her—and his hate.

Millard Graff's screams rose without end, each one a nail driving into Jess's guts.

He was not thinking when the butt of the carbine tightened against his shoulder, nor as he lined up the sights, and squeezed the trigger.

The report of the shot boomed heavily within the confines of the canyon. The carbine bullet slammed down into Millard Graff's brain, ending his agony, giving him the only gift worth anything to him—a quick death.

Chata and his warriors vanished into the dark shadows among the boulders before Jess could lever another load into the chamber of his carbine. Shoving himself backward quickly, he climbed down to the floor of the canyon. He began running as fast as he could, limping and stumbling over the rock-rubble surface. The thudding of ponies' hoofs had already started behind him when he reached the sorrel mare.

Scrambling up into the saddle, Jess kicked the sorrel so hard that the animal almost shot out from under him. He hung on tight, racing along the dry creek bed, back the way he had come. With the way sounds echoed within the narrow, tortuous canyon, it was almost impossible to be sure how close his pursuers were. But by the time he reached the end of the canyon, it seemed to Jess that they were getting closer.

Kicking the sorrel without letup, Jess raced out toward the towering stands of massive buttes, hoping to find a place where he could barricade himself and hold them off. He turned his head to see how close the Apaches were.

And saw then cavalry troopers, riding down behind him at right angles, swerving suddenly toward the canyon as the four Apaches emerged from it on their galloping ponies.

The crash of carbines split the air as Jess drew rein. He turned the sorrel sharply, raised his own carbine as he raced back. . . .

It was all over by the time he reached them. One trooper was bent over his saddlehorn, cursing, arm dangling and dripping blood. The other troopers were swinging down from their sweat-streaked, hard-driven horses, to gather around the four fallen Apaches.

As Jess dismounted, one of the cavalrymen, a big, bull-shouldered sergeant, drew his revolver and put a bullet through the ear of one of the Apache warriors. Then he kicked the other three, each in turn, to make sure they were dead, before he looked at Jess.

Jess pointed down with his carbine. "That one, the old one," he said. "That's Chata."

The sergeant turned his head and looked at Chata without expression. He said, "What d'ya know." Then he looked at Jess again and asked, "You Jess Remsberg?"

"Yes."

"Lieutenant McAllister sent us to catch you and bring you back to the post. Lieutenant said in case you don't want to come with us, I'm to put you under military arrest."

"No need," Jess told him, staring blankly at Chata's body. He felt numb. "I'll come with you."

They were still a long way from Fort Duell when it got dark. They camped for the night beside a huge mound of stones that banked up against the side of a butte on the edge of a sagebrush flat. In spite of his weariness, Jess slept fitfully, waking abruptly several times on the edge of dreams that he could not remember and did not want to remember.

He was up before dawn. While the others were finishing their breakfasts, Jess limped to the mound of stones and began climbing it. At the top, he stopped and got down on his knees. There he buried the buckskin bag containing the last remains of Singing Sky.

Then he went back to his horse and rode away with the troopers to Fort Duell, and to Ellen and her baby. He wanted to tell Ellen that he had killed her husband, finally, not in hate, but out of pity.